Vestry Vice

A Jessamy Ward Mystery

Penelope Cress, Steve Higgs

Contents

Mushy Peas

"That's twelve tins of tomato soup, three jars of Polish pickles, and seven cans of mushy peas. Everything else is on its lonesome." Barbara Vickers counted off the harvest festival inventory as the two of us packed the donations onto temporary shelves at the back of the church hall.

"I wonder who donated the pickles. Did they all come in together?" I stacked the empty cardboard boxes for recycling. Hopefully, we could reuse them after the Michaelmas service for Christmas gift packing.

"Yes, I think a parent left them after this morning's playgroup. My guess is a pregnancy craving miscalculation."

"Very probably. And the mushy peas?"

"Ah, I know where they came from. Old stock from the grocers."

"Are they still in date?" I picked up a can and wiped off a thin layer of dust from the label.

Barbara snatched it back. "It's in a can. They will last forever!"

"True." I surveyed the wondrous sight before me. Crammed pantry shelves bowing under the weight of dusty aluminium cans and glass jars. Most had labels, some more intact than others, but one small corner provided a refuge for the mystery items. These could contain pineapple chunks or mulligatawny soup. We traditionally delivered these metallic potluck gifts to the homeless kitchen on the mainland, whose cooks would work wonders with the secret ingredients. "Who would have thought that the good people of Wesberrey would have so many unwanted tinned goods?"

"They'll be of use to someone, Reverend."

"Which is more than can be said of the giant wheatsheaf loaf. I always think it's such a waste. By the time it comes off the altar, it's inedible. Still, it's tradition, I suppose. I will collect it from the bakers after lunch. Do we normally have fresh produce as well?"

"The stallholders are usually very generous. Phil will run a collection after the market on Thursday and bring up their donations."

"Great, so I think we have everything in hand. Just the school assembly left. I will sort that out with Lawrence later."

Lawrence. My heart sank a little. Recently, he had been a little distant. I wasn't sure what was wrong and, to be honest, I was too afraid to ask.

The summer had been wonderful. He had been attentive, romantic, and charming in every way. Lawrence, I discovered, owned a yellow convertible, which he kept in a rented garage on the mainland. Over some of the warmest months on record, that car took us on many adventures. Together we had unfurled our picnic mat on sandy beaches along the southern coast and eaten apples under ancient oaks in sun-dappled forests. We'd sipped cocktails in urban bars and downed cider in riverside taverns.

We bought English Heritage *and* National Trust passes and had visited every stately home and museum within a fifty-mile radius. At every destination, Lawrence was an affectionate, if awkwardly romantic, gentleman. There was one music festival at a nearby castle, where a passing shower forced us to find shelter under Lawrence's weatherproof jacket. His gallantry failed miserably. The combination of wind, and our near comical differences in height, meant that a sudden burst of rain soaked us both to the bone. But the following week of red nose and sniffles was worth it, for I have never felt stronger than I did during that blustery hour spent in his soggy embrace.

The weather turned, and so it seemed, did Lawrence's attention. At first, I thought it was because his mind had returned to thoughts of the new school year. Work on the new Academy building had started, and there was much to occupy his time.

Most of the school was a construction site and children were to be taught in makeshift port-a-cabins for the rest of the Autumn Term. Parents and pupils complained, but the promise of an indoor pool and a dance studio helped to ease their concerns. It was an ambitious plan for a primary school, but Lord Somerstone's legacy was for the creation of a community centre at the heart of island life.

It would be marvellous, but for now, it caused long working days and early nights to nurse the resulting headaches. I had barely spoken to him since work began. In fact, I had spoken to his mother more. Mrs Pixley must recoil in horror every time the phone rings with another of my desperate messages for her son. *But I miss him...*

Barbara, unusually perceptive, noticed the furrow on my brow. "He's just busy, you know. It's the hardest part of the year. He'll be settling the new kids in; preparing the older ones for their exams, etcetera. It will come good at the half-term. You'll see."

That's an entire month away! I contorted my frown into a smile. "Yes, and we're busy, too. Let's get back to the office. Rosie dropped off some vegan carrot cake yesterday, and there's no way I can tackle that bad boy on my own."

*****

A hefty slice and stiff mug of caffeine later, Barbara and I sat on either side of the study's mahogany desk, working through the church's diary for the next three months.

"Wedding bookings are trailing off as expected. I thought October would be more popular, though. The weather is still good, usually." I scrolled through the calendar on the computer as we cross-referenced with the entries in the main parish ledger.

"Oh, I'm sure there will be an upsurge soon," Barbara muttered as she flipped through the ledger. "After the hot summer we've had, I'm sure there'll be a few 'before-it-starts-to-show' bookings."

"On Wesberrey?" I giggled. "Never!"

"Every year," she replied. "Sad, really. Many of them will divorce before the bump starts nursery." Barbara hesitated. "Not something Phil and I need to worry about, though."

I acknowledged the pain in her heart. I felt it too. For some of us, love and marriage come too late for children. Though, I now know, as future goddess protector of the triple wells, that was never on the cards for me. Children, that is, not love and marriage. *Marriage might not happen either...*

"But you have each other. And married life looks good on you, Mrs Vickers. Still in the honeymoon stage three months on."

"Oh, Reverend. We are like two peas in a pod and no mistake. Though what my mother would say about her daughter living above a public house. God bless her soul. Sometimes I can feel her scorn, during the night, through the bedroom curtains. She's followed me from the cottage, bless her."

Nothing spooky about that!

"Oh, I meant to ask, how's Karen settling in? A good tenant?"

"No trouble so far. Poor thing. Still grieving. Well, I guess it's been no time at all for her."

"No, I guess it hasn't." I had badly neglected my old school friend. We had talked about her working for me as a housekeeper when Mum moved out to live in her cottage by the sea, but Karen was the first to admit that she wasn't the most domestic of women and could barely look after herself. She had welfare support to pay her rent on Barbara's old house, and for now, at least, she had a comfortable and secure home in which to grieve the loss of her only child.

Sam kept a friendly and a professional eye on her. It was early days. Now that Lawrence was so busy, I had no excuse but to give my friend more of my attention. *Note to self: arrange a Wesberrey Angels girls' night in.*

The hall phone rang. Both of us raced to pick it up.

"I'll get it. You put on the kettle. Just enough time for a second cup before I head to the Square." I elbowed Barbara out of the way.

She bounced ahead and reached out her arm to grab the receiver. "It's my job. I'm the parish secretary." She waved me into the kitchen.

"It might be a personal call." I protested.

"Then they would ring your mobile."

"Point taken. Tea or coffee?" I shuffled backwards, straining to overhear the conversation. Calls on the landline were rare these days. Most enquiries come via email. I dragged my feet as I reached the door.

"Sorry, no, we can't do the thirty-first. The church is fully booked. We have spaces the week before if that'll work? Yes, I know it's Halloween, but? Suit yourself then."

How strange? October 31st was empty just a few minutes ago. The familiar clunk of the receiver dropping on its cradle heralded the end of the call. Footsteps followed. I busied myself with the lid of the teapot. "What did they want?"

"Oh, nothing. It was a wrong number."

Good Morning, Vicar!

The crisp autumn air bit through my clothing as I rode down to Market Square. I had attached my largest pannier bag to the back of Cilla, my orange scooter. I knew I was facing the real prospect of carrying the wheatsheaf back up to St. Bridget's via the funicular railway. Sometimes the lack of cars on the island was extremely frustrating.

John and Deborah Needham, the bakers, would normally deliver the bread in their ape van, but its suspension broke driving over the unmade roads on the island's east side and was in for repairs. The Needhams were close to retirement. There was no way I was going to ask them to carry the oversized loaf up the hill. It was a mere inconvenience. I had plenty of time to make the round trip.

The tree canopies accompanying me down to the harbour were heavy with yellowing leaves. Summer was over, winter's icy blasts were around the corner, and sun-kissed memories were already fading in the long, dark nights. Rounding the final yards before the bakery, I dodged an obstacle course of puddles. Overnight rain pooled around loose cobblestones. Getting the wheatsheaf back in one piece looked less and less doable. It would be a fun return trip loaded up with bread. I pulled up close to the front door and unstrapped the saddlebag in preparation.

"Good morning, Vicar. Getting chilly, eh? Come in quickly. It's toasty inside." John Needham reminded me of a toby jug, stout and rosy-cheeked. His good lady wife, Deborah, was also short and round, with a white cottage loaf for hair. She was wrapping my enormous bread offering in red gingham cloth. The delicious, yeasty scent of fresh bakes danced around me. *Is there a mightier smell on the planet?* I wanted to pull up a chair and draw in its perfume all day.

Deborah was justifiably proud of her creation. "It's come out a treat this year. Got the oven fixed, didn't we, my love? It was catching the edges a bit for a while. No one likes a burnt bun, do they, Vicar? Can I interest you in one of these here tomato and olive loaves? Have to keep with the times, Don't we? Eh, my love, I said we've got to keep with the times."

"Right, my dear, that we do. Your sister is doing a mighty fine trade there with her new cafe, Vicar. She places a regular order with us. Happy to oblige. No eggs, though."

"Nor milk neither." Deborah chimed in a manner that suggested this was a regular conversation. "Most breads are fine. It's the cakes though. Have to keep up with the times. Don't we, my love?"

"Yes, my dear, that we do." John Needham pulled on some well-worn oven mitts and opened the oven door. "So, Vicar, there's not been any murders for a while?"

I giggled. "Nope, Wesberrey is getting a little boring to be honest."

John placed a steaming metal tray of twisted breadsticks on the counter. "Just how we like it, eh, my dear?"

"Oh yes, my love. The island was getting as bad as London. Crime at every turn. Knife-wielding gangs roaming the streets after dark. And no one wants that, now do they, Vicar?"

"No, they don't, Mrs Needham, they certainly don't." I made my excuses, muttering something about a prior engagement back at the vicarage, collected the carefully packed wheatsheaf and walked back towards Cilla. I balanced the gingham parcel carefully on her leather seat with one hand and tried to flip open the straps of my bag with the other. A familiar voice offered assistance over my shoulder.

"Good morning, Vicar! Let me hold that for you. Don't want the Needhams' handiwork in the gutter."

"Stan! Thank you. I thought I had worked it all out, but I guess I imagined I was an octopus. Wish I had more hands." I handed over the bread to the owner of Bits and Bobs, the hardware shop on the corner of Market Square, opposite my sister Rosie's bookshop cafe - Dungeons and Vegans.

"No, you just have the two, as far as I can see." Stanley Matthews was a helpful, if sartorially challenged, member of the community. Always ready to lend a sausage-fingered hand when someone was in need. His wife, Audrey, a dragon with painted talons, guarded access to Lawrence during the school day more ferociously than Smaug defended his mountain of treasure. She had been on friendlier terms with me the past few weeks. That was unnerving. Maybe she had resigned herself to our relationship, but I was wary of the truce - especially as I had no idea what had caused it.

"How's the family?" I asked.

Stan slipped the wrapped wheatsheaf carefully into the opened leather pocket. "All good, thank you. My lad's in his final year and already in full exam mode. I want him to take over the shop when he's finished his GCSEs. You know. I was thinking of changing the name to Matthews and Son, purveyors of quality goods."

Phew, the bag is just big enough. "That's a lovely idea. Though I like Bits and Bobs, it's a fun name that says what it is."

"Don't you think it's a little quirky? Audrey thinks it doesn't have enough... What was the word she used? Gravitas."

"Ooh, good word." I secured the leather straps through the brass buckles and stepped back onto the pavement to survey Bits and Bobs' shambolic shop front. It leaned cluttered with domestic hardware, brooms, buckets and all manner of useful paraphernalia, ready to fall into the square with a strong enough wind. It reminded me of its proprietor - relaxed, unpretentious, fit-for-purpose. "Perhaps you should discuss it with your son, as it's going to be his one day."

"Of course, brilliant suggestion. You're not just a pretty face, eh, Vicar? I say it to Audrey all the time. I say, that Reverend Ward has beauty and brains."

Ah, do you? That would explain a lot!

*****

I held my breath as I parked my scooter. The bumpy road back to the vicarage may have reduced the Needhams's artistry to breadcrumbs. The gingham wrapping looked stable. Afraid to look inside, I lifted off the bag and walked at a snail's pace to my front door. Barbara was there to greet me.

"Reverend, you have some visitors. I showed them into the morning room and offered them refreshments." Stepping back into the hallway, she whispered. "It's that guy off the telly, and he has a camera crew with him."

"What guy off the telly?"

"He says he's an old friend of yours. He even winked."

"He winked?"

"Yes, like he was a *friend* of yours. If you get my meaning?"

I didn't.

"You know, the one that does all those 'A Day in the Life of...' shows."

My mind was still drawing blanks.

"Used to be in Eastenders..." Barbara's frustration with my lack of recall ended when she stomped out his name. "Tobias Dean!"

Tobias Dean! My ex-boyfriend from my drama school days! Oh no, not here. Not now!

The Show Must Go On

I last glimpsed Tobias Dean through tear-soaked eyelashes as he walked towards Charing Cross station. He had dumped me. It was New Year's Eve, just after midnight, in Trafalgar Square. This cinematic moment, worthy of any Bridget Jones's diary entry, heralded one of the worst years of my life. The year ended with a road accident that would thwart my minor West End debut. I spent opening night languishing in a hospital bed. Jobless, boyfriend-less, and hopeless.

I consider myself very lucky, though. For it was in the hospital that I found my faith. Who knows? If Tobias hadn't been such an egotistical jerk, I would never have found my true calling. There had been a score of New Year's celebrations since that night. He dented my heart a little, that is all. I took a deep breath and opened the morning room door.

Barbara did not prepare me for the Adonis holding court in front of my fireplace. *Oh my goodness, he is beautiful. Bald, but beautiful!*

"Tobias!" I thrust out my hand with extra vigour to mask my melting knees. "It's been ages. What brings you to Wesberrey?"

His emerald eyes devoured me. "Jess, Jess, Jess. Look at you! Even more radiant than I remembered." His glance shot to my left hand. "And still no wedding ring, I see. Married to the job, eh?" He whisked me around to meet his crew. "Guys, this is the awesome Reverend Jessamy Ward, the sexiest crime-fighting vicar in England."

My blush burned well beyond my cheeks. Even my toes were pink with embarrassment. "Tobias, you haven't changed a bit." I wriggled free from his muscular embrace and steadied myself. "Would anyone like some more tea? I know I need a coffee."

Hot beverages ordered, Tobias returned to centre-stage. "Jess, let me introduce my team. They are the best money can buy." My ex walked over to the armchair. "This is Yemi Adongo, the hottest cameraman in the business. This two-hundred-pound mountain of chocolate beefcake makes me look good." Tobias landed a series of faux punches on Yemi's torso. "Yemi has travelled with me all over the world and been my right hand in some of the toughest places on the planet."

"Lovely to meet you. I am afraid you will find Wesberrey really boring." My welcoming smile bounced back off his sour face. Yemi grunted, tired and disengaged. Barbara appeared with some homemade cake. Hopefully, that would raise his spirits.

Tobias moved on, oblivious of, or resigned to, Yemi's mood. It was hard to tell. "And be careful what you say around Dev here. He's a master of espionage. Nothing illegal, of course. But my shows would be nothing without his talent for picking up on whispered conversations."

Dev, wearing a slim fit tee-shirt with a decal for a band he was way too young to remember the first time around, looked up from twiddling with his recording equipment long enough to engage a broad smile. "Hi there, Rev. I'm Dev Patel. Yeah, just like the Slumdog Millionaire actor, but not as wealthy."

"Pleased to meet you, Dev." I turned to the last member of the crew, a pretty frizzy-haired strawberry blonde with marmalade freckles.

"And this..." Tobias faked a chivalrous bow. "This is Amy Turner. Fresh out of film school and eager to please. We'd be lost without her. Literally. She is in charge of location and travel."

"Tobias has told us all about you, Reverend, and your crime-fighting ways. It is so kind of you to let us document your life."

"Document my what?" *I have a bad feeling about this.*

Tobias pulled my arm and guided me to the French window. "Jess, didn't you get my email?"

"Er, I think the shocked expression on my face would tell you no, I didn't. But, regardless, you certainly didn't get a reply. I need to run this past the bishop. You can't just turn up out of the blue and start filming people!"

His green eyes reached through to my heart and pulled it up into my throat. "Jess, please. We are here now. I promise you won't even know we exist. We'll just follow you around while you get permission from the big guy. If he says no, we can the lot. Sound fair?"

"It sounds manipulative." Recollections of a more controlling relationship than I realised at the time fell over themselves in my mind. "I'm not very comfortable with this. What about permission slips, waivers, etc? You can't invade an individual's privacy like that."

"That's Amy's job. She can charm koalas down from their trees. Few are immune to her methods of persuasion."

You've found a kindred spirit there then.

"We have travelled a long way, well, from Manchester, and the team are really excited about following a murder-busting priest in action. Amy has hired some crazy transport options to get us around this backwater, *and* we have rooms at the Cat and Fiddle."

"*And* I'm sure Phil is glad of the business." *Think, Jess, how can I get out of this?* "But, though I've helped solve a few suspicious deaths recently, this is Wesberrey. It's hardly the crime capital of England. I'm afraid you will find my preparations for the harvest festival very dull."

"You leave that to me. We can work out the angle later. I'm thinking we could talk about past cases, interview the culprits in prison, and speak to the victims' families. If nothing happens, we can use that footage to show how exceptional your involvement has been. Father Brown meets the Vicar of Dibley."

As Tobias talked, he sucked me into his Jedi stare. My arguments against this intrusion were ebbing away fast. "Okay, if you promise we have an absolute veto on any content and you air nothing on any platform until I get the green light from the bishop. I will want to see proof of all permissions granted as well. And you will stop recording wherever I ask. Some of my parishioners are extremely vulnerable."

Tobias planted a kiss on my unprepared lips. "Gorgeous! I knew I could count on you. And maybe…" He leaned in closer and stroked my reddening cheek. "… we can catch up. I have few regrets in life, but losing you is one of them."

My legs melted. There was an unwelcome tingle in my breasts. *This is not good. Biology sucks.* I directed my thoughts to Lawrence. The devil himself was tempting me, and I needed an infusion of goodness. *Remember the festival, remember the rain.* It worked.

"I'm sure there will be time to reminisce. Hopefully, you will have an opportunity to meet Lawrence Pixley. He's the headmaster of the local school and my *partner* in crime. He's amazingly supportive, and quite the detective."

Tobias blanched for a moment before recovering his composure. "He's your *partner*? Well, this little reunion just got a lot more interesting."

Jam and Jerusalem

Any hopes I had for some divine intervention putting an end to this television nonsense crashed a few hours later when I received a call from Archdeacon Falconer. Bishop Marshall thought it was a splendid idea! I was to give the film crew full access to every part of my daily routine.

His exact words were: "It could be a wonderful recruitment tool for the church. Help us shed the crusty image of vicars sipping Earl Grey with the local WI." Given that the Women's Institute was more famous now for their suggestive nude calendars than their jam making, I challenged that was racy enough. My protests fell on stony ground.

Mum had popped over for an early supper. She greeted my latest news with her default parental concern. "I hope you aren't thinking of rekindling that flame," she mumbled over a pea risotto. "Remember how much that idiot hurt you the last time. I know Lawrence isn't as... exotic, but you have a good man there. And he's besotted with you."

"I've seen that Tobias Dean on his TV shows." She continued. "Pretending he's some hard man; going into prisons and ganglands, courting danger like he's a gangster, not a former soap star who appeared in one Guy Ritchie movie. He's too pretty to last one night inside a cell. It's good television, but seriously, we all know he sleeps in the nearest five-star hotel overnight."

"He'll be slumming it at the Cat and Fiddle then," I joked. "You never said you watched his shows."

Mum's detailed knowledge of my ex-boyfriend's career history was troubling.

"I suppose I should check them out. Get a sense of his reporting style."

Mum shrugged. "How long is he here for? Fingers crossed, no one shows up dead. The last thing this place needs is any more drama."

I watched Mum chase a loose green ball around her plate. "He didn't say how long. I'm sure he will get bored with my parochial life and move on quick enough."

"So, will they be escorting you to the seance?" Mum stabbed the errant pea with her fork.

Oh no, I've forgotten about that! "I will have to make some kind of excuse. I shouldn't be going, anyway. What would Bishop Marshall say?"

Mum almost choked with laughter. "Well, if Muriel is on form, it will put tea with the WI in the shade, that's for sure!"

Muriel was a local medium with a loyal following. My aunts claimed she was a rare creature with genuine talent, though her gifts were a little on the theatrical side for their tastes. After months of pleading for guidance from them on how to channel my recently discovered powers, my Aunt Cindy had organised '*An evening of clairvoyance with Mystic Muriel*'. How this soiree would help me understand my own ability to talk to dead people was quite beyond me, but I had resigned myself to never understanding my aunt's mysterious ways.

The 'evening' had completely slipped my mind. It was happening tomorrow at eight.

*****

I had tossed and turned all night, trying to work out how to prevent Tobias from finding out about my date with the supernatural. The result? Dark shadow moats around my sleep-deprived eyes. I prayed Amy was also a trained makeup artist.

15

I might more productively have prayed for a giant sinkhole to form in the churchyard behind me. Then I could jump into the depths of hell, which would be considerably less painful than what the morning would bring. When the crew arrived at eight sharp, they buzzed with local gossip and talk of the evening's special audience.

Amy was an excited giggle of finger-dried curls. "Reverend, you have the most interesting community here. I did lots of research before we arrived, of course, but I learnt more about the history of this small place in the pub last night. I mean, I saw nothing about your family being witches and all. Wow! And you a Church of England vicar and all that. Must make for fascinating family get-togethers."

"Technically, no one in my family claims or denies being a witch. That's not a term I have ever heard any one of my aunts use." As I lifted Hugo off the kitchen table, I caught Amy's knowing glance. *Yes, I have a black cat, so what?* "And to be honest, I am a little disturbed this is being discussed in the local hostelry."

I was also a little surprised. I hadn't thought about Phil or Barbara discussing this side of my past. But they were the beating heart of Wesberrey. Barbara had lived here her whole life. Rumours were rife. Of course, they knew about the Bailey girls and the legend. We had discussed it at the first PCC meeting. Everyone was just too polite to mention anything to me directly. *Does everyone talk about it behind my back?*

"Once they heard we were filming you, it was hard to get people to shut up. You have a cult following. This is going to be the best show I've ever made. I am thinking of a limited series even." Tobias plonked himself on one of the kitchen chairs. Placing his trainers on the wooden bar at the end of the table, he pushed the chair back on its rear legs. The urge to topple him over rose within me. *God, help me resist temptation.*

"And," added Amy, "it seems old flames abound on this little love island. Yemi met an old lover, too. Didn't you Yemi?"

Yemi, doing his best not to engage with the conversation, merely growled in agreement.

"So, the problem I have is which bit do we cover first?" Tobias reached down to stroke my fluffy familiar. "I thought you were allergic to cats?" He shook his bald head. "Anyway, the boys will have set up soon and, well, I had planned on a simple piece to camera, then a quick tour of the church, you know. Ease us into the shoot gradually and see what comes out. But now I want to get you in a dark room with a spotlight and ask you some more probing questions ahead of the seance tonight."

"The seance? You know about that?" *Time to lie, Jess, or back out, or both. The Boss will understand this is a necessary evil.*

Amy tutted. "Silly Billy, Reverend, there's a poster advertising the event in the pub's saloon bar. And there was a leaflet in each of our bedrooms. I mean, it is happening in their event room. How could we miss it? And according to Yemi's old beau, you're the guest of honour!"

Hotline to the big guy in the sky - sinkhole needed NOW!

"So, er, who is Yemi's old beau?" *Change the subject. Distraction. Diversion.*

A deep grunt emanated from behind a floating camera, the extension of which was attached to Yemi's waist. "Kat." he coughed.

"Kat? Kat Pringle? The lady who makes corn dollies and lavender wreaths?" Kat Pringle was a new-age hippie who lived next door to my Aunt Cindy. She was creating some 'offerings' for the harvest festival. I had only spoken to her a few times on market day. She always had the most beautiful stall covered with delicate, pretty corn figures and wall hangings.

Yemi shifted his feet. "Yes, she said she was into all that now. It's been a few years. We'd lost touch. I didn't know she lived here."

"Small world, eh?" smiled Tobias, "and the lovely Kat told us lots about Mystic Muriel *and* her witchy neighbour. Who, I understand, is none other than your Aunt Cindy! Goddess of the wind and sea or something like that."

Amy pulled out her smartphone and started swiping. "I wrote it all down. Protector of the Wells of the Triple Goddess. One of those wells is under the church font, right? Can we see it?"

My stomach churned. Pandora had been busy. The box was open, and the lid jettisoned into the sea that I was drowning in. I wasn't even sure Hope remained. *I can't breathe!*

I lied about needing to brush my teeth and rushed upstairs. The only place of comfort was the floor behind my bedroom door. I crouched down into a sitting foetal position and rocked.

I needed to send a distress signal up to my boss. I needed Lawrence. I needed a way out.

The Bell Tolls

Throwing supplication to the heavens may not have resulted in desired bolts of lightning, but my timeout in quiet prayer calmed me down. I returned to the kitchen with renewed acceptance. The Lord works in mysterious ways. Perhaps he had a greater plan in train beyond any understanding I could muster. I had to trust in his mercy and loving embrace, whatever lay ahead. And make sure that Tobias and friends didn't find out anything else.

The first scheduled appointment to film was my routine visit to the cottage hospital. A short walk through the graveyard to care for the sick. A normal vicar-type activity. Nothing witchy or supernatural about that. In fact, it could offer the ideal alternative angle. They seemed to like cats. Their viewers would love cats. I would lead them to hundreds of the furry little creatures.

"Right, next on my to-do list is to feed the famous Wesberrey Chowder. You must have heard of our feral cat colony? You'll get some great shots."

Equipment and tinned food gathered, we traipsed out the back door, leaving Hugo mewing behind us. "So, what's his name? Lucifer? Beelzebub?" Tobias joked.

"Hugo," I replied, opening the garden gate onto the back lane that connected the vicarage to the graveyard.

PENELOPE CRESS, STEVE HIGGS

"You named him after one of your other exes? I feel slighted. Tobias is a noble name for a cat."

I took too much pleasure seeing how this irked him. "True. Your name just didn't spring to mind, I guess. Here, let me know when you are set up. They come quickly once I ring their bowls."

On queue, the moss-covered headstones disappeared under a carpet of tortoise-shell and tabby bodies, slinking and stretching in the morning sun.

"Dev, did you get that? We can use their calls to add texture to other atmospheric shots. I think we need to come back at night. Find the magic in the moonlight." Dev gave a thumbs up. He had been so quiet I forgot he was there. Silence is an excellent quality to have in a sound engineer, I supposed.

Next stop, the Wesberrey Cottage Hospital. The combined superhero efficiency of Barbara and Amy meant Sam had already granted her permission to film on hospital grounds and a selection of willing and waivered patients lined up for me to visit them. Martha greeted us at reception.

"Welcome! Dr Hawthorne said to escort you to the day room first. Old Mrs Jeffries is a huge admirer of the Reverend here and is desperate to sing her praises. Mind now, she's ninety-three, and a little deaf, but has all her faculties. You should do a documentary on her life. She worked at Bletchley Park during the war. They were a special breed that generation and no mistake. My father fought in the Caribbean Regiment. Though he never spoke about it. Heroes, all of them." Martha smoothed down her lilac tunic and led the way.

Mrs Jeffries and I had a lovely chat. Her rheumy eyes laced with tears as she spoke of her late husband. It was reality television gold. Tobias's glee was contagious. There was some comfort in seeing how the camera's attention lifted the patients' spirits. I took advantage of a brief break for the crew to film scenes of the hospital wards and grounds to pop in to see my best friend in her office. Alone.

Sam greeted me with a heavy sigh from her leather chair. "Jess, you've really lost the plot this time. Why do you have a film crew following you around?"

"I could counter that with why did you agree to let them in your hospital?" I swung around in the matching swivel chair on the other side of her desk. The simple act of spinning around the room helped to ease my anxiety.

"Stop that! What are you, four?" Sam took an elastic band from her desk tidy and flipped a pink paper clip in my direction.

"Ouch" *Who's being childish now?* Unarmed, words were my only defence. "Hippocratic oath means nothing, eh? 'Do no harm' ring any bells?" I carried on spinning, dodging a barrage of paper clips from my bespectacled opponent.

"Talking of bell ringers—""Were we?"

"You brought it up."

I suppose I did. "Truce?"

Sam nodded.

"What about the bell ringers?"

"Well, several of yours have presented here with repetitive strain injury. It's quite common. I suggested they conduct a risk assessment. Which they did and, well, they want to meet you to discuss their working conditions." Sam slid her glasses up over the bridge of her nose. That was always a tell that she was serious.

"They're volunteers!"

"Yes, but they want to talk to you about what safety measures you can put in place to prevent further injury."

"Okay, I'll meet them. Don't want them suing the church for negligence. Or me personally, for that matter." *I have enough problems right now.* "Sam, I want your advice, so can I be candid?"

21

"Of course. Better be quick though before Mr DeMille wants me for my close-up."

"Haha, hilarious. It is about Tobias, though. Did you know we used to date? It was a long time ago. I was in the last year of drama school and, well, the break-up hit me really hard. And then, he turns up uninvited with a film crew. His plucky PA finds out all about my 'witchy' family, and they're convinced they've got a BAFTA-winning show here. The Bishop thinks it will be great, but he doesn't know about my family's past or present. They want to learn more about the sleuthing but, Sam, what if they find out about, you know, *my gifts*? Then there's the seance tonight. I knew it was a mistake..."

"What with Mystic Muriel?" Sam laughed.

"The cameraman, Yemi, he knows Kat Pringle. Seems she's been saying all sorts."

"Oh, Kat Pringle has a loose tongue. I think she's harmless, but she has few kind words for me. Ms Pringle isn't a great believer in modern medicine. She has an online shop selling all sorts of herbal remedies and potions." Sam waved a dismissive hand in the air. "She can't trade them on the market. That's why she makes those wreaths and stuff. They're a front for her more nefarious activities."

I thought about my Aunt Pam's spell room and all the jars of 'special' ingredients. I was sure Cindy probably had a hidden chamber behind a secret panel or something. Maybe there was a coven on Wesberrey after all. My stomach fluxed again.

"I should back out, shouldn't I? This isn't going to end well. I can feel it?"

"Well, let's look on the bright side. Maybe that film crew will unmask these charlatans? That will be a service to both of us." Sam was a scientist. Despite all she had learnt about me and my family, she struggled with alternate world views. I was still struggling with everything myself.

"I fear it's a dangerous game to play. What if they unmask me?"

"Look, Jess. I don't have a rational explanation for your abilities, however, just because science can't explain it yet doesn't make it supernatural. I mean, there's a lot to be said for herbal remedies. After all, we make aspirin from willow bark. It's the intention, right?

You and yours mean no harm. Kat Pringle and her kind are new-age fraudsters who play on people's vulnerabilities with their misappropriation of other cultural traditions like runes and dream catchers and the like. Crystal healing? I mean, come on!" Sam jumped to her feet and paced the room. "And as for Mystic Muriel! Taking advantage of people's grief. I can't think of anything worse."

A sharp knock on the door stopped her tirade. Tobias's sun-kissed egg face appeared seconds later.

"Dr Sam Hawthorne. Your secretary said now would be a good time for an interview? I was thinking we could start in the morgue. It will make an outstanding backdrop."

Sam paused. "By all means, set everything up, and I will be down in a few minutes." Tobias's grin lingered, Cheshire cat-like, long after his actual face disappeared behind the closing door. Sam walked over and pushed it firmly shut. "Girl! You never told me he was that cute! I mean, I usually prefer my men to have hair on their heads, but that smile? He's adorable. Have you told Lawrence?"

A sudden urge to change the subject leapt from my lips. "He's really busy with the plans for the Academy and all that. Don't you want to freshen up your make-up? Re-comb your ponytail, perhaps?"

I went to stand, but Sam pounced jaguar-like forcing me back into my seat. "You are avoiding him, aren't you? It's a sin to lie, Reverend Ward, remember? You're not worried about being unmasked. You're worried about being undone! Did you? You know. You dated before you went all Sound of Music on us." Sam searched my face for evidence she was right. I tried to stare through her to the wall behind. "Oh my! You did!"

Sam clapped and danced around the room.

"Don't tell Lawrence!" I begged. "That was a lifetime ago before I knew any better. I am a very different woman now."

"Jess, you have my word. But one word of advice. Nothing stirs a man more to the chase than thinking his prey is unattainable. Tobias is on the prowl. I can smell it. Just be careful. You or your story, that man is on a mission. He will do anything to win."

Talk of the Town

The afternoon brought some respite from the constant whirl of the camera. After lunch, my first appointment was with an engaged couple to discuss their wedding plans, and they flat out refused permission to film. Not that I could relax. At least when they were my annoying companions, I knew what Tobias and his crew were up to. Now they roamed unfettered across Wesberrey, hunting down their prey in a cavalcade of hired scooters. It was market day. My cup of anxiety overflowed with thoughts of traders and tourists telling tales about Wesberrey's curious vicar.

I was to meet the crew later at Rosie's cafe for a non-dairy cream tea.

I arrived to discover that the crew had been interviewing the customers at Dungeons and Vegans for most of the afternoon. Stanley Matthews had handed over the charge of his shop to his son once he returned from school and was now sitting at one of the bistro tables outside, looking very dapper in a clean shirt and tie. I almost didn't recognise him.

"Afternoon, Vicar. I'm up next. They want to talk to me about when we apprehended poor Rachel's killer. You made quite the splash when you first arrived here, eh?" Stan chuckled, largely to himself. I sensed this was a joke he had used often when retelling his version of events.

I sat in the free seat next to him. "We made quite the team, eh?"

"That we did, Vicar. That we did."

A few moments later, Rosie appeared with a steaming cup of oat-milk coffee. "Here," she said, "I figured you would need this."

I wrapped my fingers around her offering and thanked her for this life-giving elixir. "Been busy?" I asked.

"Yes, you should have a film crew follow you around all the time. It's been great for business." She pulled up a chair from the next table to join us. "So, Mum tells me you're going to that seance. Have you completely lost your mind?" I arched my eyes towards Stan, indicating this was not the time to have this conversation. Rosie carried on with her interrogation, despite, or maybe because of, the fluffy microphone boom suddenly dangled above her head. There was probably a camera behind me. "Don't you think the Church Of England would frown upon such nonsense? You are a pillar of this community. You have to protect your reputation."

"They're friends of our aunt. It would be impolite not to go. And the Church is more progressive these days. More open to other beliefs. I will be there merely as an observer. I shan't be taking part in any conversations with the dead."

"And cut!" Tobias's voice boomed across the bustling Market Square. "Jess, that was perfect. If you and your sister could just run that again? Yemi, I think the setting sun is giving us better light from the street."

Stan raised his chubby hand. "Mr Dean, what do you want me to do?"

"Mr ...?" Tobias stopped.

"Matthews," Amy whispered from inside the shop.

"Yes, Mr Matthews, just do what you did before."

"But I didn't do anything," Stan replied.

"Exactly. It was perfect." Tobias stepped out to join Yemi and Dev in the street. "Sound ready? Camera? And... action!"

*****

The unobtrusive, fly-on-the-wall, 'you won't even notice we're here' film crew drew a sizeable crowd of stallholders and visitors. They circled behind Tobias and his team, straining their heads to see what was going on. Our casual sisterly chat was 'just' run again half a dozen times. The hubbub from the gathering onlookers caused Dev problems with the sound. I only took a few sips of coffee before it went cold.

"Right, that's a wrap!" Tobias turned to face his audience. "Thank you for your patience, ladies and gentlemen." A voice asked for his autograph. Followed by another and another. Tobias obliged with a full-on charm offensive to every request. He was in his element. They appeared to love him almost as much as he loved himself. There would be no more filming that afternoon.

Yemi and Dev methodically packed up their equipment and mumbled to each other about recharging batteries and themselves before the night's festivities. I noticed they had mini trailers attached to their scooters. Something similar would have made getting the wheatsheaf back to the vicarage a darn sight easier. *Note to self, pop into Sal's and see what other accessories I could buy for Cilla.*

Amy thanked Stan for his time and remade arrangements for an interview before taking his vacated seat at our table. "Tobias has been talking to Netflix and Sky. The BBC isn't biting, yet. But they will. We expect a feeding frenzy over this one."

"I'm sorry, Jess. Ms Turner. But I have to attend to the shop. I guess I have a hot date with Mystic Muriel tonight. Speak later, Sis." Rosie kissed me on the cheek as she passed. I felt like my entire world had walked off with her.

"Amy, erm, I'm intrigued. How much do you know about me and my family?"

"Tons! You're descended from a long line of female goddess protectors. Something to do with fertility and protecting life, crops etc. and there's always the same pattern in each generation. There are three sisters; one has three daughters, one a son, and the other is destined to take on the mantle of the godmother. I think that's right. So, in this generation, that's you. I've already met Luke, so Rosie is in the clear, and from what I hear your other sister, Susannah, has three daughters. Though, she's shacked up with the chief of police in one of those swanky apartments on the harbour front. Seriously, this series is writing itself."

My life swirled in front of me. "Wow, you have been doing your homework. Anything else?"

"Oh, I've only got started!" Amy slapped her thigh like a pantomime principal boy. "You moved away when your father topped himself. And yet, since returning you have all inherited lots of cash and been able to set yourselves up very nicely, thank you. Add to that your penchant for catching murderers, this is going to be huge! Watch out Kardashians, I'd say."

"And don't forget the cats," I added feebly.

Amy's freckles glowed with delight. "Yes, everyone loves cats!"

*****

As the gathered hordes returned to their business of shopping and seeing the sights, I left Tobias, wrapped up in a blanket of adulation, to catch a few words with Kat Pringle before she closed her stall.

Her purple hair was easy to spot. The thought of her and Yemi together made for an intriguing image. Yemi was tall, dark, with an air of geek. He had an athletic build. My guess was that he was a runner or hurdles guy at school. Kat was probably watching from the stands. If this was an American teen movie, she would be the outsider, dressed in gothic black, who professed to be anti-establishment and non-conformist but went home to a fluffy pink bedroom. She had now found inner peace by wearing long, flowing tie-dyed robes and embroidered cheesecloth. A silver pentagon hung around her neck.

"Reverend Ward! I was wondering when you were going to pop by. Excited about this evening? Muriel has an amazing talent, but from what I hear," she whispered, "so do you."

"Kat, I don't know what Cindy has told you. But with the TV crew here, and everything…"

She handed me one of her corn dollies. "Do you know the history of the dolly?" I shook my head. "Well, traditionally they're made with the last sheaf of the harvest. They capture the spirit of the corn and, keeping them safe, ensures a good crop for the following year. It's important to remember our roots, eh, Vicar?"

"Yes, and to be grateful for God's bounty. I suppose that's why we have the bread wheat-sheaf on the altar at the Harvest Festival service." We both smiled, each respecting the other's faith and our interconnectedness. The corn dolly in my hand was beautiful. Not at all figurative. It was, instead, an interesting triple moon design, most unusual and very intricate. Kat certainly had skill and flair.

"It represents the phases of the goddess. Maiden, mother, crone."

"I think I went straight to crone." I laughed. "How much?"

"To you, Reverend? Nothing, it's my gift. You know, the crone represents wisdom, strength, resilience. The ultimate representation of female energy. This world is too obsessed with youth. We need to embrace the feminine divine of the crone. She has the power to heal us all."

"Thank you." I was genuinely grateful. "I understand you know Yemi Adongo. Funny him turning up here like this."

"Yes, seems we both have fated reunions with past loves." Kat checked the clock over the Guildhall in the centre of the square and began to pack up. I did what I could to help.

Remembering my earlier conversation with Sam, I asked, "So, do you sell these online as well?"

"Yes, amongst other things. Take one of my cards." She pointed to a small stack on the front of the table. As I reached across to take one, a pale hand sporting a spider web tattoo stretched in and knocked the pile onto the cobbles.

"Fraud! Copycat! New-age wannabe!"

I turned to see a red-faced young woman with jet black hair and matching make-up picking up the last few items on the stall and hurling them across the square.

Kat wrestled with the stranger. "Shelta, you're making a scene. Stop it!"

"I'll stop it when you stop stealing my stuff! My life! Why can't you leave me alone?"

A Night Like This

F ists and corn offerings flew in all directions. It took several stallholders to tear the women apart. As peace resumed, both parties, shaken by their encounter, dusted themselves off and shook hands in an uneasy truce. I offered to facilitate a three-way conversation to help resolve their issues back at the vicarage. Each declined and marched off their separate ways, leaving me behind with a head full of questions.

This altercation had something to do with the local supernatural, paranormal, 'witchy' community and my aunts know all the players and their respective issues with each other. I tried calling Cindy, but her phone went straight to voicemail. So instead, I made a beeline for Pamela's house. It was the closest anyway, and time was pressing.

"Hmm, so Cindy was unavailable then?" Pam huffed as she placed a cotton doily on the side table next to me.

I couldn't lie to her. "Well, Kat Pringle is her neighbour, so she was an obvious first choice. But I really appreciate that you don't speak in riddles. By the way, did you hear that Hugh Burton got the part in the Ron Howard film he was after?" I realised it had been a while since I last sat down for tea with my aunt. It would be good to make small talk before I started firing off questions.

Pam settled herself on the floral armchair opposite me. "Yes, he called me with the news a few days ago. He's flying out to Mumbai next week."

"Ah, so you are in regular contact then?"

"I wouldn't say regular," she preened, "He calls every other week. Hugh's a busy man."

"Yes, yes, he is. Do you know what the film is about? Has he let anything slip?" I wanted to keep the conversation flowing, but I was also curious - this was arguably Hugh's big break into Hollywood.

"Something colonial. Passage to India type of thing. He did mention he would be wearing a lot of white linen..." I detected a slight swoon as she spoke. "But that's not why you're here, Jess. Come on, spit it out. Byron will be back from the garden centre soon."

"Cindy has organised this seance thing for tonight, and I don't know if you've heard, but somehow, I've got a TV crew attached to me. I had to be very cloak and dagger to sneak off here unnoticed. Anyway, that's bad enough, but earlier I witnessed a brawl between Kat Pringle and another witchy type called Shelta? I guess you know them both." My aunt nodded. "So, what I want to know is, do I need to be worried?"

"Oh, I don't think Shelta Lee means you any harm at all. Though I guess there's a chance of getting caught in the crossfire." I gestured to my aunt to carry on. "Shelta has a magic shop off the high street of a tiny hamlet on the other side of Oysterhaven. I say hamlet, maybe it once was, but really, it's Oysterhaven now. Anyway, it's a lovely little place. Unassuming. The building itself is probably fifteenth century, has a low ceiling, wooden beams. Tiny. Anyone over five foot has to bend to get through the door. Very cute. Not a lot of passing trade, so she set up an online shop."

"I see, and along comes Kat Pringle and steals her customers!"

"That's not all of it," Pam leant forward and, though no one else was anywhere near, spoke in a conspiratorial tone. "Kat Pringle is one of these new-age hippies. Discovered Wiccan back in the noughties and attended a few retreats. Thinks she knows it all. Don't get me wrong. She has some good knowledge and sufficient skill for a newbie. But the Lees have wisdom from the old country. Shelta can trace her gypsy bloodline back to her Irish Pavee roots, and she is rightly proud of her heritage. Like us, she has cunning passed down through generation after generation. Mother to daughter. Aunt to niece."

"So, she also has gifts?" I put my tea mug back on its crocheted resting place. I was keen to hear Pam's answer.

"I doubt it. She has wisdom. She can probably enchant. I understand she had studied hoodoo and has branched out into root and bone work. If her faith is strong, I imagine she can be very powerful, but that is not what we do. I mean Cindy and I dabble on the side. I prefer herbs, and Cindy does energy work. I'm sure Cindy has told you, you have to find what works for you."

Will I ever hear this and not want to run screaming to the hills?

"And Muriel? Where does our local medium fit into all this?"

Pam took a sip from her mug. "Oh, Muriel sees dead people."

*****

It might have been the promise of an evening of psychic entertainment or the compelling sideshow of a TV crew, but the event room to the back of the Cat and Fiddle was fit to bursting with a thirsty audience. Phil had enlisted extra help from my nephew, Luke, and his girlfriend, Tilly, to help Barbara and their regular staff behind the bar. It seemed the whole of Wesberrey, was here. Well, nearly everyone. My mother was noticeably absent, as were some older members of the community. I was surprised to see my churchwarden, Tom with Martha, the hospital's administrator, chatting to each other in the far corner. Tom's partner, Ernest, obviously deemed this one piece of nonsense too far to join him.

I recognised two tall figures at the bar. "Sam? You never said you were coming? In fact, I thought this type of thing was preying on people's misery." Sam avoided my glare and busied herself with an invisible speck of dirt on her glasses. I twisted my playful sneer into an exaggerated smile. "And Leo, fancy seeing you here. Long time, no see."

"Well, Reverend Ward, business is quiet at the moment. How could I miss tonight? Maybe some of my old clients will make an appearance!" A rare undertaker's joke. Leo Peasbody's usual sombre face allowed a slight twitch in the right corner of his upper lip.

I accepted Leo's offer of an alcoholic beverage and walked with Sam to find a seat. My best friend looked radiant in a figure-hugging red dress. I had always envied her ability to wear beautiful clothes. She had the height of a supermodel and legs that went on for days. It was hard not to feel dumpy in her presence. "So, have you spoken to Leo about making your relationship more, er, well an actual relationship?" Sam had enjoyed a very casual friends-with-benefits arrangement with the willowy undertaker for several years.

"Perhaps," she sniggered. "I don't like to admit that you were right, so don't push me on it." We found some spare seats to the right of the velvet draped podium at the front of the room. "No Lawrence? I knew you didn't want him to meet the hunky Tobias. Jess Ward, you are a minx!"

"I am no such thing. He has a dinner meeting with the architects in Stourchester and will get back too late. I am seeing him tomorrow. The crew plan to do some exterior shots of the school. They will meet then."

"If you say so."

"I do." I don't know why I was being so defensive. I had called Lawrence earlier and told him everything. Leo's return saved me from any further teasing.

I scanned the room to see who else was present. I recognised the Needhams, the Matthews, Aunt Pam and Uncle Byron. Rosie sat with Tilly's father, Buck. They made such a cute couple. Avril and Verity Leybourne, the town's hairdressers, had positioned themselves front and centre. It was a full house.

I could make out Kat Pringle's purple head over on the far left. Several rows directly behind her glowered Shelta Lee. Cindy was talking on the stage to a velvet-cloaked woman I took to be Mystic Muriel. It was an impressive gathering, and a lot bigger than my usual Sunday congregation.

I nudged Sam's elbow. "Perhaps if I start talking to the dead at Sunday service, I could get the numbers up?" I quipped.

Sam giggled. "I think that would be very enterprising of you. Ssh, they're dimming the lights, it must be about to kick off."

Muriel took her seat on the raised dais, and Cindy stretched out her hands to welcome us all.

"Brothers and sisters, in this world and the next. Thank you for coming together here tonight. As you can see, we are joined here tonight by a wonderful TV crew who are following my beloved niece, and your wonderful parish priest, around for a week or two." The assembled crowd murmured and looked in my direction.

"But that is not why any of you are here." More mumbling. "I am delighted that we have with us tonight a woman with an incredible gift. I have known Muriel for most of my life. She would hate me to remind you all how many years that is." The cloaked figure bowed in the chair, her head lowered so we could not see her face. "I present to you, the marvellous Mystic Muriel!"

Cindy strode off the stage and signalled for the remaining lights to be turned off. All that remained was a simple spotlight illuminating Muriel centre stage. She raised her head and turned it slowly from left to right, before resting in the middle where she closed her eyes.

Muriel breathed in and out. Instinctively, her audience joined in with her rhythmic breath. In and out, in and out. Everyone was silent, the only sound - our own heartbeats. In and out. In and out. A muffled cough from the back row jolted us out for a moment, but Muriel kept a steady pace to which we returned. In and out. In and out.

A soft voice floated from the stage. "Please, everyone, close your eyes. You are safe. The spirits are here, and they wish to join us." *In and out.* "Close your eyes and ask them in." I took a sideways glance at Sam. Her eyes were closed. *In and out.* I closed mine too.

Muriel continued. "I can see two people. A couple. They have come together. They have come to see their babies. I have the letters A and, this is unusual, I am hearing a V? Could it be Victoria?"

"No, no, it's Verity! Avril, it's Mum and Dad! It's for us. They've come for us!"

Muriel told everyone we could now open our eyes. Verity was pulling Avril up from her seat. She was so excited. Avril was less sure.

"Do you have any questions for your mother," Muriel asked, "or your father? He looks very proud."

Avril pulled her sister back down in her chair. "Is he? Is he really? Ask him. Go on?"

"Avril, don't," Verity implored. "Why do you still want to fight him, even now?"

"He says he is impressed that you have your own business. He only wants you to be happy. And you are happy together. You provide a valuable service to others with your work, and he is proud of all you have achieved."

Avril crossed her arms. "This is a hoax, he would never say that. He wanted me to be like him. Go to university, Become a teacher! It's lies, all lies." She sobbed.

Muriel remained calm. "Your mother wants you both to know they are always with you. Please ask her something only she would know."

Verity raised her hand.

"We're not at school!" Avril pulled it back down again. I had never seen her so tetchy. The twins often bickered playfully, but the mention of their father had triggered something. If this was a hoax, it was in danger of backfiring.

Verity ploughed on. "Ask Mum what she gave to us for our birthday the year she passed."

Muriel paused and at the very least pretended to listen for an answer. "She bought you both tickets to see Dirty Dancing - the Musical. You had your own box. No one puts baby in the corner."

Both sisters gasped, turned to each other and hugged.

The room erupted. Muriel took a few minutes to regain order, but soon we were moving on. More messages came from the other side and appeared to be recognised by the receivers as genuine. Throughout the lights remained dimmed, and repeatedly we were asked to close our eyes.

I was impressed but remained unsure how this performance would be useful to me in my quest to understand my special talents or the role I was to play. At least, no one from our family had popped by for a celestial chit chat. Tobias would have interesting footage, but nothing on me.

One more time we were instructed to close our eyes. If this went on any longer, I was in danger of falling asleep. I was sure somebody was already snoring behind me. Deep breaths. In and out. In and out. *In and out.*

"Jess? I have a message for Jessamy Ward."

I opened my eyes and raised my hand. Part of me was convinced this was a put-up job. Only my mother calls me Jessamy. I could sense Cindy's hand in this. "Yes, I'm here."

Muriel rolled her head back and forth. Her breathing grew more laboured. Her chair rocked.

There was another voice calling out across the room.

Death! Death! Death!

Muriel screamed. "Death is here! Death is in the room!"

Cindy rushed on stage and clapped her hands to signal the lights to go back up.

Muriel stared out into the audience. "One of you is going to die!"

"Okay, okay. No need to panic. Everything is fine." Cindy looked around for support, but the room was in chaos. I grabbed Sam's hand, and we ran to the front.

Muriel had fainted. Sam checked her pulse and worked to revive her. I took Cindy's place at the front of the stage and begged for calm.

Death! Death! Death!

That voice echoed around the room. *What am I supposed to do?* In my heart, I asked whose death, but there was no reply. Out of the corner of my eye, I could see Tobias motioning to Yemi to keep the camera rolling. It was time to call in the cavalry.

VESTRY VICE

"Ladies and gentlemen. Let us pray..."

When in doubt, let go and let God!

It Tolls for Thee

"You sure you'll be okay on your own?" Sam hugged me goodnight at the end of the path. After attending to Muriel and assessing all was well, she and Leo had escorted me home. Now they needed some alone time.

"Yes, I'm sure. I've called Lawrence. He will be here shortly. Are you certain you didn't hear that voice?" I had convinced myself, in the hours that followed Muriel's histrionics, that it must have been a recording, a theatrical trick.

Sam winced. "No, we've told you repeatedly neither of us heard anything. I don't know what you heard or why, but we heard nothing." A final hug and I turned towards my front door. Sam called up the path. "We'll wait here till you put the light on."

I turned and thanked them for their concern. I really was fine, just confused. A disembodied voice crying, Death! Death! Death! is a pretty pointless warning. Whose death? Mine? Muriel's? Someone else? What was I expected to do with that information? I had heard such things before and they had prevented nothing. Neither did these premonitions ever help me find the murderer. So, what was I meant to do now, just wait for a body to turn up?

The only thing I could do was to put on the kettle for a cup of tea and throw together a couple of sandwiches from the leftovers in my fridge. Lawrence would be in search of a snack. He wasn't even here yet, and I was already wishing he wouldn't stay too long. I felt drained.

Maybe it wasn't him that was tiring of our relationship? Maybe it was me? I spent the next twenty minutes talking myself in, out, and around that notion. A pointless activity, because the moment he knocked on the door, I knew how I truly felt. I wanted him to stay forever.

It had kept my mind off who was next in line for Leo Peasbody's specialist services, though, which was a bonus.

"I can't stay long." Lawrence leant down to kiss me, his face cold from the night air. "I have a breakfast call with the school accountants."

"Ooh, the life of a high-powered executive." I snuggled into his chest. "I'm glad just to see your face. The film crew will be here again at eight in the morning. Though I think they will find the meeting with the bell ringers rather boring after tonight's events."

"Talk about too much excitement. We have the harvest festival assembly on Friday. I will have to wear a tie."

I pushed back and laughed. "You always wear a tie!"

"Well, then maybe I won't. I could mix it up a bit for the camera." Lawrence stroked my hair. All my tensions slid down my body as he smoothed his hand along my neck.

There was that tingle in my breasts. For the right man this time. I wanted Lawrence in my arms, in my bed, in my life. Here was where I belonged. He was my present and my future.

"Remember, Tobias and the gang are doing their preliminary shots up at the school in the afternoon."

"You said he was an old boyfriend. I don't have to beat off the competition, do I? I am prepared to fight for you, you know. I did judo at school. Yellow belt." He squeezed me tighter and nuzzled the top of my head. It was comforting. Sometimes our height difference had its advantages.

"You don't have to fight for me. Every cell in my body surrenders. I love you, Lawrence Pixley."

"I love you too, Jess Ward."

*****

The morning after the crazy night before brought with it - aching joints (I'm getting old); a ridiculously bright-eyed, over-enthusiastic TV crew; and a band of miserable ringers.

I met the St. Bridget's Bells in the dining room. I thought the more formal setting would convince them how seriously I took their health and safety concerns. The solemnity of the conversation failed to prevent Tobias and Amy from stifling giggles behind the camera as the group talked about hand stroking the sally, or backstroking the tail. *Some people are so immature!*

When the meeting finished, Tobias invited each member of the Bells to film a vox pop piece to camera in my study. This process meant that my office was out of action for the rest of the morning, so I retreated to the kitchen.

Amy flurried in behind me minutes later. "Tobias has had the most wonderful idea. The social media grapevine is buzzing with tales of how you were there when Kat Pringle played fisticuffs with Shelta Lee. Such a shame we missed that. Anyway, Kat mentioned before the show how you had offered to mediate between them both, and Tobias thought, regardless of what they said yesterday, we should make that happen. So, I've tracked down Ms Lee, and she's game."

"When would we do this? I'm going to the school to finalise the assembly this afternoon? You were going to interview Lawrence, take ground shots, etc."

"Oh, if Kat Pringle is good to go, that will have to wait. A rematch between Wesberrey's own Glinda and Elphaba? Pure TV gold. This is such an exciting project."

Without waiting for any further response, Amy skipped back to the study. The reality of what Tobias had tricked me into shaped ominously in my mind. I had to talk to the bishop myself. There was no way this programme could ever see the light of day. *It can't be too late to stop this nonsense!*

Hugo was mewing by the back door, so I picked up my phone and walked out into the garden with him. I scrolled down to the B section of my address book. *I should have done this at the beginning.* Archdeacon Falconer was probably too excited about the prospect of positive television coverage to express my reservations properly. I was psyching myself up to hit dial when an incoming call vibrated in my hand.

It was Cindy.

I hesitated just a beat too long. The phone went to voicemail. I knew I had to call my aunt back, but I also knew in the pit of my stomach this was bad news.

Death! Death! Death!

Cindy rang again.

I took a deep nasal breath and said a small prayer in my heart, hoping it wasn't a member of the family. "Hi there, aunt! What a surprise. How can I help you?"

"Jess! Please come quick. Dave's on his way. Kat Pringle is dead!"

*****

"Well, that explains why she wasn't returning my calls." Amy packed her notebook into her pink Prada bag.

"I don't think you guys should come with me. It's a crime scene."

Tobias threw a black leather bag filled with cables and other small pieces of equipment on the kitchen table. "From what I hear, I should be able to appeal to Inspector Lovington's vanity. It usually works. And he is shagging your sister. So, he has to want to please you too." He swung the bag over his shoulder. "Jess, your life is one hell of a rollercoaster ride and a televisual gift from the gods. I am going to make you a star!"

I have to knock that crowing smirk off his face.

"Dave owes me nothing. And please, don't use that word to describe my sister's relationship."

Tobias took both my hands. "My sincerest apologies, it's just I remember a time when you weren't so prudish." His thumbs stroked the back of my knuckles. His head tilted in a coy manner.

I pulled away.

"I'm not interested." I snapped, "And I have no desire to be a star. In fact, I was just about to call the Bishop to ask him to rescind his approval."

"Be my guest." Tobias headed to the hallway. "But a little dickie bird told me that Bishop Marshall is planning to attend your boyfriend's little school assembly on Friday." He winked at Amy, who trotted behind him. "Remember the adage, *all* publicity is good publicity."

Lavender and Straw

The coastal settlement on the furthest western point of the island where Kat Pringle lived, next door to my aunt, is a remote and difficult place to find. Travellers Bay is beyond civilisation unless you count the old military base. It is the perfect hideaway for those who wish to escape from normal life. There are few signposts to guide your journey and much of the road past Stone Quay is an unadopted dirt track. It was a long way to go to be turned back by the police, but Tobias insisted I led the way.

The scenery on this side of Wesberrey is barren but beautiful, an eerie landscape of sand dunes shaped by the rolling winds of the past. We had little time to enjoy it. I was desperate to offer solace to my aunt, and perhaps Kat's spirit had hung around to talk to me. I couldn't express this to my companions, though, especially Yemi, who kept stopping to capture picturesque scenes for potential future edits. He appeared in no hurry to get to his former sweetheart's house.

Dev was monk-like, as usual. He was a curious chap. On our first meeting, he was friendly, but since filming began, he had barely spoken two words. Even after the seance last night, he had kept his head when, to misquote Rudyard Kipling, all around him were losing theirs.

Yemi and Dev's lack of interest, though, was more than made up for by Amy and Tobias's overzealousness. Their lack of respect for the recently departed woman disturbed me. A woman they had been keen to interview. A woman who had once dated one of their colleagues. A woman who had met an untimely end. Kat Pringle could not have been much above forty years old. To them, she was a story, an angle, a lead.

To me, she was my aunt's neighbour, a recognisable member of my parish community, and possibly someone's daughter, sister, or even mother. As always, I wanted to know what had happened to her and how I could help.

We arrived to find PC Taylor tying off streaming blue and white police tape around the boundary of Kat Pringle's home. "Reverend Ward, Inspector Lovington requested you go straight inside as soon as you got here." I dismounted Cilla. Tobias was quick to fall in behind me. PC Taylor barred his way. "The Inspector wishes to see the Reverend alone, sir. Now please wait here, if you don't mind."

What a relief! I thanked the constable as I ducked under the tape. Dave was waiting for me in the doorway. "I see you have your own entourage these days."

"Trust me, if you want to order them back to the mainland, you'll have my full support."

"Sadly, freedom of the press and all that malarkey, as long as they aren't impeding my investigation, there is little I can do. You need to refer your request to a higher power."

"Oh, I've tried. God's helpline seems to be busy right now."

Dave guided me to the back of the bungalow. It was similar to Cindy's in its general layout. Decor-wise, it was worlds apart. My aunt's home had a chic bohemian vibe. Kat Pringle's was a kaleidoscope of pink and turquoise patterns, hanging crystals, and dream catchers. There were kitsch curios on every available surface. Straw covered the kitchen table and corn dollies in various stages of completion lay in boxes all around.

Everything was chaotic. I was so absorbed in her decorating choices, I missed the moment when we crossed the threshold into Kat's bedroom. Seeing her lifeless body resting on the bed took me by surprise. She looked peaceful, like an anime version of Sleeping Beauty, her purple locks delicately arranged on her pillow. Everything around her was pink and fluffy. No pentacles or dragons in here, just a herd of sparkly unicorns. The room smelt of lavender. She wore a floaty white nightdress and, on her head, sat a glittering tiara.

Dave closed the curtain. "Go on, do your thing."

It was pointless to protest. To be honest, I felt it was my duty to see if I could help. I pulled up the chair from her dressing table and lifted her stiff hand in mine. "Can Cindy join me? I'm not sure I can do it alone."

Dave shook his head. "She said it's down to you now."

No pressure then. I took a deep breath.

I had met Kat, so I recognised her voice in my head. She was here, though it was impossible to make sense of her jumbled words. Not sure how to initiate a conversation with the dead woman's spirit, I figured I should just start talking to myself in my mind. I asked her to tell me what she knew.

Kat's thoughts rushed unfiltered out of my mouth. Her words became mine. There was no delay, no opportunity for interpretation.

"It was dark."

Dave stood behind me, hanging on to every word. "That makes sense. They killed her during the night. We can tell from the state of rigor mortis. Anything else?"

"I couldn't sleep. Nothing new there. I always struggle. My mind is constantly whirring. I'd drunk some valerian root tea and was listening to a sleep app on my phone."

Dave coughed. "Hold on, Jess. Are you repeating what she says, or is Kat Pringle talking through you?"

I disengaged to answer him. "She's talking through me. Don't ask me how it works because I don't know."

"Wow! Carry on."

"Wow! You really said wow? Please let me concentrate."

I settled back down and reopened my inner chat function. *Kat, I'm sorry for interrupting you. This is all very new for me. Please tell me everything you can remember.*

She continued. "I can't sleep, you see. So I use this app. It plays thunderstorms, crashing waves, and crackling fires. Very soothing."

"There were no headphones on her body, and no sign of her mobile either." Dave scribbled in his notebook.

Kat talked on, oblivious. "They've done the research, you know, into how the sound of rain helps us to relax and heightens our creativity. Some say the white noise gives our minds something to focus on that is non-threatening. Others say that back when we were cave dwellers, we knew predators would seek shelter in a storm, so they wouldn't be after us for a midnight snack.... Reverend, I'm dead, aren't I?"

Yes, Kat, I'm afraid you are. Did you see who did this to you?

"No," Kat replied. Her voice was shaky. Uncertain. The reality of her situation dawning on her.

"No, what?" A reasonable question. The inspector was only getting half of the conversion. I ignored him. Something told me I had little time left.

Kat, think. I've seen them do this on Criminal Minds. I get that's a weird reference right now, but... Just relax and try to remember what you saw, felt... Tell me, what could you smell?

"Lavender. I love lavender."

Anything else. Anything out of place?

"The sea. Sea salt." I shook my head. This wasn't getting us anywhere. Everything on Wesberrey smells of the sea, and her whole house reeks of lavender.

What can you see?

"It's dark. I can't see. Something covering my face!" Kat panicked. My pulse quickened. I could see what she could, which was nothing. "Air. Air! I can't breathe! The smell of the sea is so strong. Am I drowning? What's holding me down? The pressure... it's crushing my face. My nose! Help! Please help me! No, no, no! I don't want to die..."

Dave touched a gentle finger to my shoulder. "We believe they smothered her with a pillow."

I gasped for air.

I am so very sorry. Anything else?

"Nothing. It's like daylight, but there's nothing. There's nothing here!" My voice cracked over her words.

This was hard. Kat Pringle was alone and scared.

Kat, can you see me?

I was curious. I had to ask.

"Yes. Yes, I can. Oh my! You are holding my hand. Who put the tiara on my head? I only wear that on special occasions!"

I think it was whoever killed you. Do you want me to take it off?

"No. It was my favourite. I look so pretty."

Do you have any other messages for me? Perhaps to pass on to a loved one?

"No, there's no one left. I want to go now. I can see a light."

Please, stay a while longer. Help us catch who did this to you.

"I have to go. It's okay. Really it is."

I remembered how Cindy responded last time.

You're right, it's time. Go in love, Kat. Thank you.

A shiver passed through me.

Dave placed a hand on my shoulder. "Has she gone?"

I swallowed hard before answering. My mouth was desert-dry. The tears in my heart, though, could flood the Sahara.

"Yes. She's at peace now."

Uncovered

D ave drew back the curtain and opened the window. "I heard somewhere, you're supposed to let the soul out.

"Yes, some people believe it allows their family to come in to take them home. I hope so. Kat sounded so alone." I crossed her hands over her chest. "She was right. She does look very pretty."

"Yes, almost like this was staged." Dave flipped open his notebook again and jotted something down. "You'd never think she had fought for her life."

"But she did. Someone wanted her to look her best."

Dave tapped the notebook against his chin. "Hm, someone? Probably the killer held her in some affection. Or they felt remorse?"

"A bit late for such sentiments," I mumbled. "Are there any real clues to who did it?"

"The glass in the back door shattered onto the inside mat, so it looks like they broke in. I will get forensics to do a thorough search of the land around the perimeter. We might find a footprint."

"I'm sorry I couldn't get any more information. This gift of mine is pretty pointless."

"If I thought that, I wouldn't have let you try it. There may well be a clue in what Kat could tell us. We just don't know it yet." The inspector guided me out of the bedroom. "Miss Pringle was an interesting character if her home is anything to go by."

"Yes, she was. I was only talking to her yesterday. She got into a fight on her stall with a woman from Oysterhaven. Shelta Lee. Put her at the top of your suspect list."

*****

The conversation turned to my sister Zuzu, who was visiting her daughter Freya in Durham as she settled into her new digs for her final year at university.

"Seems they went out clubbing together. It's good to let your hair down once in a while, I suppose." Dave's eye twitched. A sign I had learnt meant he was anxious about something.

I placed a comforting hand on his arm. "Don't worry, she adores you. I've never seen her this crazy about a man. She'll be back soon."

"Maybe we should have found a place in Stourchester. You know, city life and all that. I'm afraid she'll find me and our life too pedestrian."

"From what I've heard, my sister loves being the little hausfrau in her penthouse apartment overlooking the harbour. She's never really had a base. Security. You provide all that and are great in bed, so I understand. Zuzu overshares." I smiled. "Dave, you really have nothing to worry about. But your concern is very cute."

"Hope I'm not interrupting." Tobias pounced the second we emerged into Kat Pringle's garden. "Can I borrow the vicar for a second?"

Dave, slightly pink of face, welcomed the change of conversation, shrugged, and went to speak to PC Taylor.

"Ah, so that is Inspector Lovington. Handsome man, the camera will eat him up. That moustache is a choice, though. Very Errol Flynn. Anyway, what is going on with you two?

I thought he was your sister's boyfriend. Yet there you were, all close heads and whispering behind closed doors. And windows. Dev noticed you drew the curtains."

"Did he? I was simply praying for her safe journey onwards. That is my job, you know." I pointed at my clerical collar.

Tobias winked. "Are you sure that's all you were doing?"

I recoiled at the suggestion. "My relationship with Inspector Lovington is professional and above board." I suspect I protested too much. Tobias was quick to pick up that my righteous indignation was hiding something.

"Okay, you were doing more than saying a few prayers. Are you and he?""No!"

"Well, you were up to something, unless you always blush so prettily over... Hold on, if you weren't up to no good, then you were helping with the investigation! Of course! Now, what can you offer an experienced chief of police that an army of forensics can't?"

He looked skyward for inspiration. "You can see dead people!"

I dragged Tobias further along the path, away from the rest of his crew. "I don't see dead people."

A tilt of the head confirmed his thought mill was grinding overtime. "No, but you can hear them."

I cannot tell a lie. Not a barefaced one, at any rate. There are some things I knew my Boss would have a hard time countenancing. I decided if I couldn't tell the truth, then my best recourse was to plead the fifth. I remained silent.

"You're not denying it, so my hunch is correct. Jess, that is amazing! Is it just a dead people thing or can you read minds? Do you know what I am thinking right now? Go on, try me."

I folded my arms, kicked out my hip, and stared him down.

"Jess, the psychic priest! Man, do you have any idea what we could do with this? There hasn't been a good ghost-whisperer on TV for years. Combine the true-crime angle with that sexy uniform of yours, and I smell hit, hit, hit!"

"And I smell the muck they spread on the fields." I chose to ignore the sexy uniform comment.

Tobias stood, confused for a second. "Fertiliser? Oh, manure! Hilarious, Jess. See you are so funny! Wesberrey's own Dawn French. I have to see if Dev picked up anything…"

"Picked up any what?"

I scuttled behind as Tobias walked off towards his soundman, who sat crouched down by the fence, twiddling knobs on his equipment. Tobias lifted one of Dev's headphones and whispered something in his ear. Dev grinned.

This can't be good.

Dev took off his cans and handed them to Tobias. My legs became like cooked spaghetti. I grabbed the fence for support.

"Ouch!" I caught a sliver of rough wood in my finger. *That smarts!*

"Reverend Ward, are you hurt?" Amy rushed to my rescue.

"Not really, it's only a splinter." This was an opportunity to make a clean getaway. "Maybe my aunt has some tweezers. I won't be long."

I ran to Cindy's, tears sliding down my cheeks. The pain was not in my hand but in my heart. Tobias had found the golden goose. And my life was about to be ripped apart.

*****

"Darling, hold still." My aunt hovered over me with the mini silver pinchers. Eagle-like, Cindy swooped in and plucked out her prey. "There, all done." She patted me on the head. "Such a good girl."

"Aunt Cindy, I'm not a child!" I sucked the end of my finger to relieve the pain. I realised the irony of this petulant image. "Thank you."

Cindy settled herself across the room. "How are you feeling? A little dizzy, perhaps?" "It was just a splinter." I caught her tender expression and knew she wasn't talking about that anymore. "My legs gave way. I... I think they recorded me somehow when I was channelling Kat."

"Ooh, you are progressing fast. Channelling is very advanced. Did she use your voice, or did you use hers?"

"Mine, I think. Do you mean there might be a future me that will sound like the deceased? Isn't this bad enough already?"

Cindy smoothed down her navy cheesecloth top. "Darling child, I believe you need a strong cup of tea. I'll put the kettle on. You rest. Put your feet up."

My aunt glided towards the kitchen.

All the tea in China wouldn't be enough to drown out the screaming in my head. I felt obligated to find Kat's killer, but the last thing I wanted was to provide more sensational footage for Tobias. Despite all his sweet talk, I knew he had no interest in me. He was interested only in what I could give him. Right now, he believed I would bring him fortune and fame. Such a dream made him dangerous.

Tobias wasn't the only danger. Dev was obviously a master of covert surveillance. Tobias had mentioned his ability to secretly record people. Now they had me channelling on tape. That evidence had to be destroyed.

My thoughts drifted to the cameraman. Yemi was strangely unaffected by Kat's death, but he had worked with Tobias for years. Maybe he had learnt it was best not to offer up any vulnerability. Or perhaps his relationship with Kat was fleeting, and the reality was that he hardly knew her. Even if their relationship had been serious, it was a long time ago from what I knew. Did it end bitterly? Could Yemi be the murderer?

There are only two probable suspects from where I sat, very comfortably in fact, on my aunt's chaise lounge - Yemi and Shelta. I was desperate to visit Shelta, but that was impossible with a film crew on my tail.

Maybe I would have to sit this one out.

Maybe...?

Multi-Coloured Moods of Love

A frantic pounding shattered my quiet contemplation. From the kitchen, I could make out Cindy's soothing tones comforting another woman. The visitor's voice was weak but familiar. As they drew closer, I swung my legs down from the chaise and readjusted my blouse, ready for duty.

"Don't worry yourself now, there's no way you could have known." Cindy led the way into her lounge. "Muriel, have you met my niece?"

I stood to take the medium's quivering hand. "I don't believe anyone formally introduced us. Please, sit down, you look like you have had a terrible fright." I guided Muriel to the sofa and sat beside her. Cindy took her position in a chair opposite.

I had only seen Muriel the night before, spotlighted on the pub's stage, cloaked in confidence and velvet. The frail old woman who shrank before me was a marked contrast. She struggled to speak. Her eyes flitted from me to my aunt and back again. I implored Cindy to provide some context to this situation. I thought Muriel lived in Oysterhaven. Why was she here, and why was she so upset?

"Jess, darling. Muriel was staying over in my shepherd's hut in my back garden." Cindy responded in a matter-of-fact style that verged on the frustrated. In my defence, this was the first I knew about a shepherd's hut, but then I had never ventured to the ends of my aunt's backyard. She could house a full-on hippie commune there, and I would be none the wiser. Cindy was always economical with information. If I had asked, point-blank, do you have board and lodging on the premises, then I am sure she would have mentioned it. Possibly. My other aunt, Pamela, or even my mother, would have assumed I knew. They assumed I knew a lot of things.

"Oh, of course, I see." I returned my attention to the trembling woman beside me. "Have you just heard about Kat? Awful business, isn't it?"

"I warned you. I warned you all. You heard it too, didn't you?" Muriel remained agitated.

I hesitated.

Cindy answered on my behalf. "Of course she did. I feel partly to blame. We should have discussed it last night. But, Muriel, you needed to rest and, well, Jess, darling, you wouldn't have given it any credence."

"I might have..." Proud indignation choked my words back down. "I asked Sam and Leo if they had heard anything. And they didn't." I coughed. I felt my arms folding into a crossed position and caught them just in time.

"Of course they didn't. Darling, why would you seek validation for your experiences from those who cannot offer it?"

Cindy made a good point. The obvious reaction to hearing phantom voices should have been to speak to the ghost whisperers. A significant part of me was still uneasy with this side of my heritage. I wanted to embrace it. I was desperate to use it for good. There was much comfort in helping the recently departed move on peacefully, to know that there was a place for them to go. But I struggled with random warnings of doom and destruction.

It was time to face my fears head-on. "Muriel," I squeezed her hand gently. "Tell me everything."

"Won't the TV people be looking for you?" she whimpered. "I saw them circling Kat's house. Like vultures. Only word for it. I overheard one of them. The girl. Trying to sweet talk the constable into letting them inside."

Muriel's crepey skin felt fragile under the soft stroke of my thumb. "Why were you at Kat's house?"

"To invite her for lunch, of course. I thought she would relish a cooked meal eaten alfresco. Such a pretty spot by the hut. And it's a glorious day, is it not?" A visible lump rose in her throat. "I sensed Kat needed company. Your aunt provided me with a well-stocked hamper of goodies. Could never manage it all myself. Eat like a bird these days. I have very little appetite. One of the trials of getting to my age, I suppose."

Muriel's wrinkles provided perfect valleys for her tears to meander through. "I figure I'll be joining poor Kat for lunch on the other side soon enough."

"Plenty of life in you yet." I offered, only to be met with a melancholy shake of the head.

"My time is near, dear. I can sense it. At least I will go confident into that sweet light knowing I can always pop back to visit." A serenity flooded Muriel's face.

"So, you saw the police and knew Kat was dead?" That seemed a bit of a leap to me.

"Not exactly. I saw the police and knew something was wrong. Then I saw the film crew, so I crouched down, well I bent over. I have terrible trouble with my knees. Anyway, I hid behind the buddleia. That has come on beautifully this summer. Still plenty of flowers."

"True, Kat was creating quite the oasis." Cindy rose and mimed putting a cup to her lips. "I think I need to re-boil the kettle. You must both be parched!"

"Do you have Earl Grey?" Muriel called after, then taking a deep breath, she flipped over my hand so that my palm was facing the ceiling. "I understand you have the gift." She traced her bony index finger along its lines. I went to pull away, but her grip was remarkably firm for a woman who seconds earlier was predicting her own imminent demise. "Hush now, dear. You have many questions. Let me help you."

"Maybe another time. You've had an awful shock."

"No time like the present, I find. Especially when I don't know how much time I have left. Well, neither do you, dear. But your lifeline is strong, so I wouldn't be too worried, just yet."

That's comforting to know!

I shrugged my acceptance. This was less painful than dodging Tobias's awkward questions, though they would come to find me sooner or, preferably, later.

"You must accept your fate, dear. It is an honour to be the next Protector. I see you have misgivings. I know you are confused." My anxiety softened as she spoke. Muriel had a reassuring tone, even if her words offered little solace. "You fear you cannot serve your God and the Goddess. But, my dear child, they are one and the same. God is both father and mother to us all. They are the source of all that is. We are their children. If you cannot see the feminine in your Lord, the bounty, the life-giving force, then he is unworthy of your dedication."

"But he is all that is and ever was."

Why do I have to defend my faith?

"Exactly, my dear." Muriel patted my hand. "He is. She is. They are." She smiled and looked out towards Kat's cottage. "We earthbound souls cannot fathom the whys and wherefores. It is not for us to question. What I know is that they choose their servants. The special ones whose job it is to support and to guide. As in every family, we have our roles to play. You and I, and others like us, are the ones our parents trust to corral the other siblings back home safely. This gift of yours is not at odds with your religion, it is the source of your faith. Think of the good work you do shepherding your flock."

"I guess, but I know many priests who make excellent shepherds and don't have dead people talking to them over breakfast!"

"Maybe not, but they hear the divine. It is the same frequency. Ah, time for tea." My aunt re-entered with a tray of late morning goodies. "Please, Reverend, you be mother."

Milk poured and biscuits distributed, I was keen to go back to the butterfly bush. "So, what did you overhear behind the buddleia?"

"Well, the young woman was asking the policeman if she would let the cameraman sneak in the back door to take a few shots of the body in the bedroom. I knew Kat lived alone, so it had to be her. And the use of the word body suggested she was dead. She was livid when the constable refused. She marched off like a fury. I think she made a phone call, can't be sure, but she was talking to someone else as she stormed off."

"Do you remember what she said, exactly?"

"Sorry, I lost my balance, and it was all I could do to not be discovered. But she was frustrated, angry even. As soon as she was out of sight, I raced over here."

The Last Rose of Summer

I wanted to question Muriel some more, but the unmistakable image of a film crew on the hunt appeared on the horizon outside my aunt's picture window.

"Looks like we have company." Cindy brushed a few wayward crumbs from her clothing and headed to the door.

Muriel's pearly complexion faded to ash. "Reverend, they cannot find me here." There wasn't time to compute why she was so afraid of being caught on camera. Last night, she was anything but shy. However, I figured no lady wants to be filmed without at least a touch of lipstick, and she was grieving a friend. I ushered her into the kitchen with an earnest promise that I would coax them away at the earliest opportunity.

I joined my aunt in wait behind the front door. "Let's get them away from here as soon as possible. Muriel needs some time to gather herself together."

"Bless your heart." Cindy beamed. "I say we open before they knock. That'll spook them."

And it did.

*****

"You *are* psychic!" Tobias winked. "Yemi, tell me you got that on film?" Yemi shook his head. "Never mind." Tobias barged into the tiny hall. "I say we forget about going to interview the boring headmaster this afternoon and stay here. You can call your boyfriend and postpone, eh, Jess? Ah, the legendary Cynthia Ward. Wow, Yemi check out the lighting in this room. I want to catch this stunning creature in all her natural beauty." Tobias swirled my aunt around. "May I say, Miss Ward, you are exquisite. Yemi, pan these pictures on the wall here. These were you, right? When you were younger? Man, oh, man! Wesberrey just keeps on giving."

My ex's brash entrance infuriated me, but my aunt appeared delighted with his flattering words. She danced around the room like a young girl going to a prom. "Tobias Dean! You are a silver-tongued devil. Please come on in and have a seat. Let me make you all some tea. Jess, this will have gone cold by now." Cindy grabbed the tray swiftly and spun her way towards the kitchen. She nodded at the three cups as she passed. Now I understood her response. It was a distraction.

My turn to pick up the baton. "You must all be starving? Make yourselves comfortable whilst we throw together some lunch." I waited to make sure they were all comfortably seated before joining my aunt in the kitchen.

Muriel had already left.

I reached across to the windowsill to pick some parsley to garnish the plate Cindy was preparing. "Aunt, why did Muriel stay in your back garden last night?" I whispered over a salmon quiche.

"Because the last ferry had already left? Jess, darling, sometimes you really are dim. How did you think she was going to get back to Oysterhaven at that time of night?"

"Good point. So, Shelta Lee? Is she camped out in your backyard as well?"

"Of course not. She would have stayed with her aunt and uncle."

"Oh, she has relatives on the island? Anyone I know?"

The kettle clicked itself off. Cindy stretched past to pull fresh cups from the shelf in front of me. "I should think so. They made that pagan wheatsheaf for your ever so Christian harvest festival altar."

"You mean the Needhams? Small world."

"Yes, that it is. Darling, can you get the milk from the fridge? I think our guests have waited long enough."

*****

Amy poked at her plate, separating the pink salmon from its yellow eggy casing. "Erm, Reverend. I don't suppose you could have a word in that handsome detective's ear for me and convince him to let us film the body?"

Yemi swallowed hard. "Isn't that disrespectful? She was someone, you know."

"And someone you knew. This must be very hard for you." Amy's request appalled me, and I wanted to show Yemi that I understood his pain.

"Oh, Kat and I, that was a long time ago. It's just we should have more respect for the dead."

"Yes, we should." Tobias took his plate free hand and slapped his cameraman's back. "Amy, put your enthusiasm back in your Prada handbag. Some things are off-limits,"

"And macabre!" Piped up Dev from his position cross-legged on the floor at Yemi's feet. "Much more effective to put sound over haunting monochrome photographs. Perhaps the police will give us access to the ones the forensic team takes of the crime scene. We can blur out the gory details."

This was one comment too far for my aunt. "Kat Pringle was my neighbour. Maybe, she's just an interesting development to you or even a distant memory." She glared at Yemi with such force, he choked on his pastry crust. "But she was someone with the capacity to love and be loved. A soul whose time on this glorious planet someone's monstrous private agenda cut short. For what else is the taking of another's life, if not the most heinous crime possible."

"Now, I understand you have different priorities," Cindy continued, "but this is my house, and I would like you to eat up and leave as quickly as you can."

*****

Duly chastised, Tobias and crew packed up and left in a flurry of, I would like to believe sincere, apologies. With no further leads to follow here, they were returning to their original agenda and heading up to the school.

I assured Tobias that I would follow behind as fast as Cilla would carry me, but first I wanted to say a proper goodbye to my aunt. Cindy and I watched them from the gate scoot off back along the coastal road.

"Well, it's a good thing you kicked that Mr Dean into touch. Lawrence is a much better man." Cindy conjured a small set of pruning shears from the pocket of her smock top and snipped away at a fading bush. "Here, the last roses of summer. I think I should give these to Muriel."

"They are beautiful. I know this is unthinkable, but Muriel *was* very jittery. I understand her upset at losing a friend, but you don't think there's any more to it than that, do you?"

"Jess, darling. You need to learn to trust your intuition more. What do you feel? Not what do you think?"

What I feel will not hold up in a court of law! "I don't *feel* she's a murderer, but she could have been avoiding the police as much as she was avoiding the cameras."

"Perhaps. Though I ask you this: Why come to me in such a state? Why not clear her things out of the hut and wave her goodbyes through the window? Act as if she knows nothing about what happened and slip away as quietly as possible. After all, deep down at the bottom of the field, she would have seen and heard nothing."

I had to see this hut before I believed that it alone provided a convincing alibi. Though traipsing across a grassy lawn alone in the dark seemed an unlikely activity for an octogenarian. "How did she walk down there? There are no lights that I can see."

"Very observant. I have a little golf cart rigged up for guests. But I drove Muriel out there myself. And before you ask, it's safely stored in the shed."

"Are you sure? Have you checked?"

"Darling, I don't need to. It makes one hell of a racket when you drive it. To be honest, I think it's also not long for this world. There is no way Muriel or anyone else could have driven it anywhere without waking up half of Travellers Bay."

I needed to make this journey for myself. "Let's go now then. Take those blooms down before they wilt."

Cindy sighed her agreement. "Alright, on one condition. I drive. It's a bumpy ride."

*****

As the cart threw me around, dodging sandy mounds and grassy knolls, I realised that the terrain did not lend itself to moonlit, cross-country dashes. The cart, despite its age, made quick work of it. In what couldn't have been more than a minute, though it felt a lot longer, we arrived at our destination. On foot, I imagined it was at least a five to ten-minute walk. *Not impossible, but...*

The hut itself was utterly charming. About twenty-foot long, it stood proud on an area of hard standing nestled under one of the few trees on the site. Cindy had painted the external wood cladding duck-egg blue and the trim white. Two picture windows flanked the stable door in the middle, each dressed with matching shutters and a cutesy flower box. Railed wooden steps provided easy access. To the side, a semi-circular rattan chair set invited guests to keep warm around a low-level cast-iron fire pit.

"How much land do you own?" I asked my aunt as we climbed out of the cart.

"Oh, only about two and a half acres. As you can see, most of it is sand and scrub. There is a second cabin over the small ridge there. Solar power has been the game-changer, to be honest. Some people hitch up tents here in the summer, but now I can get more into glamping. The only property with mains connectivity is Kat's place."

"Kat Pringle was your tenant?" My enigmatic aunt was frustrating. How am I supposed to know what question to ask in order to elicit an unknown piece of information? *I don't know what I don't know.*

"Yes, did I not mention that before?"

"Er, no!"

"Well, it doesn't change anything, does it?" Cindy ascended the wooden steps and knocked on the door. "Muriel, it's only us."

There was an eerie silence. My heart beat a wild counterpoint to the anxious thoughts drumming around my head. "We didn't pass her on the way. Do you think she is okay?"

Cindy knocked again.

"Can you hear rustling?" I leaned in closer to the hut.

"Muriel, are you okay?"

A few seconds later, a slightly flushed but perfectly healthy mystic guest opened the top half of the stable door, almost taking the delicate heads off the blooms in Cindy's hand.

"Pfft, of course, I'm okay. Can't a lady use the potty in peace these days!"

Peach Melba

Roses housed in an empty jar, Cindy and I dallied for the obligatory cup of tea and polite conversation before heading back to the main house. Cilla was hopefully still where I had left her, outside Kat's house. The visit satisfied me that Muriel was not a killer. It would take considerable strength to hold a pillow down over a healthy woman's face for long enough to kill her, especially if she fought back. Robust as Muriel was, why would she choose such a precarious form of murder when she could have used poison or even stabbed her, both of which would have required less physical exertion?

And Muriel didn't have a motive, as far as I could see. Pam said Kat was a wannabe with no psychic abilities, and Muriel didn't appear threatened by my gifts, quite the contrary. It was, therefore, unlikely that she believed Kat was a danger. *Unless Muriel has another secret?*

I found Cilla as expected under the careful watch of PC Taylor.

"Good afternoon, Constable. Have forensics been yet?"

"They're still inside. But the coroner has given the all-clear to remove her body to the cottage hospital. Leo Peasbody will be here soon with his horse-drawn wagon."

"I hope you can contact the family soon to make funeral arrangements. I'm happy to help in any way I can."

PC Taylor adjusted his helmet's jaw strap. "Keep your friends away? That young lady made quite the nuisance of herself earlier. I didn't fall for her lines, though, Reverend, but this is a crime scene, you know."

I patted him on the elbow. "I understand completely. And has the Inspector left for the day?"

"Yes, he went into town to interview Miss Lee. I told him she was staying with her cousins." He preened.

"Ah, yes, the Needhams." I flung a trousered leg over Cilla's saddle and put my key in the ignition. "Right well, I'd better get off. They are filming at the school now."

PC Taylor raised a hand and pointed to his head. *My helmet!* "Oh yes, safety first!" A few seconds later, suitably attired, I drove off to rescue Lawrence.

As often happens in September in England, we were experiencing a mini heatwave. This Indian summer could last a couple of weeks, days, or even a few hours. Thunderous storms often followed these temperature highs. The real question was, when would it break? Hopefully not until I reached the shelter of the school.

I pulled into the playground, which was now a car park for the contractors working on the improvements. The poor kids had nowhere to let off steam during their breaks. The result would be restless children and frazzled teachers. *No wonder Lawrence is so preoccupied.*

Removing my helmet, I took a beat to fluff my hair, using the reflection of the reception's glass door. Inside, I could see Audrey pacing around her lair. Her manicured hands played with the charms hanging from her gold bracelet as she walked, every few seconds checking the time on the school clock. I took a deep breath, pushed heavily on the door, and strode in to meet my nemesis.

"Audrey! Just point me in the direction of the film crew, and I'll head straight there."

"Er, they're with Mr Pixley." She had bitten most of the red lipstick off her bottom lip. "They said they wanted me next. I'm not sure how I feel about being on camera. I suppose to the likes of you this is like water rolling off a duck's back."

The likes of me? I'm an Anglican priest, not one of the Kardashians!

"I'll wait here with you then." *Or I could offer an olive branch?* "Better still, I can hold the fort whilst you refresh your lipstick. You'll want to look your best. They're talking about international syndication."

"Er, thank you, Vicar." Audrey combed her painted claws through her hair. "I'll get my makeup bag from the staff room."

Cosmetics in hand, she scurried down the corridor to the ladies' toilet. I took sentry duty at her desk. I could feel the power coursing through my veins. From my post, I could terrify children and adults alike. Demand dinner money with menaces and hold gym kits hostage. I was the keeper of the class registers. The fierce protector of the head. The guardian of the stationery cupboard. With great acrylic nails comes great responsibility.

Amy's shrill tones cut through my megalomania. "Reverend Ward! We thought we'd lost you. Your boyfriend is cute, cute, cute. Audiences are going to love him."

"Well, I love him, so why wouldn't they?"

I've never declared how I feel to anyone other than Lawrence, and I choose to come out to Amy, of all people!

"Aw, you're too sweet." Amy dropped her clipboard on the reception desk and arched her fingers over. Joining them together at the knuckles and stretching out her thumbs into a V-shape, she pumped this heart shape back and forth on her chest. "Gives us all hope if you can still find love at your age."

At my age?

"Right, no rest for the wicked, as they say. Have you seen the woman who was here earlier?" Amy spun around to check the waiting area. "She'd be a shoo-in for Princess Fiona if your local am-dram society ever does Shrek the Musical."

Audrey's freshly coiffed head loomed over Amy's left shoulder. "I don't do theatrics. I prefer Zumba!"

Awkward, yet sinfully satisfying.

*****

The rest of the filming at the school went without incident. I caught sight of some rushes as Yemi reviewed them, and I have to admit Lawrence looked gorgeous on camera. Audrey, despite her nerves, also did Wesberrey proud.

My only concern was that Tobias and Lawrence had *bonded*. Seems they had discovered a mutual admiration for James Bond movies. Whilst I could see Tobias fancied himself as a bald 007, Lawrence, being a fan of the womanising secret agent, licensed to kill, was quite the surprise. How this topic had come up in conversation was an even greater mystery.

"My new pal, Lawrence here, has suggested we eat at the posh French place down the road." Tobias hung off my boyfriend's neck like they had played rugby together for years.

"The Old School House? It's very expensive." I protested. "I have the parish council meeting this evening, not sure I have time for a proper meal before then."

"Well, I have to feed the troops. Yemi is prone to getting very hangry if he doesn't get his three square meals every day."

"Hangry? Oh, you mixed hungry and angry, very clever." My smile curled around my gritted teeth. "Well, we had better get a move on. Don't want Yemi turning green and busting out of his clothes, now do we."

*****

We arrived at the restaurant as the manager pulled back the bolt on the entrance to open for the first service. It was still bright outside. We had a good couple of hours before sunset, and the parish council meeting.

For ease and efficiency, we agreed to go straight to the main course. You can tell a lot from people's menu choices. How adventurous they are, how predictable. Of course, any analysis of character traits needs to be approached with caution. They could have already eaten and are being polite ordering again, or they are unwell or have allergies and so on.

But, from a base assumption that they have a healthy appetite and are not harbouring any eating disorders, their decision to order omelette and chips versus omelette with a salad garnish can be very revealing.

When Tobias and I were at drama school together, we studied Stanislavski and even attended a Lee Strasbourg workshop once. An effective method for getting into character involves a question-and-answer session in a group. Everyone in the session takes a turn in the hot seat. They pulled one chair out to face the rest. When it was your turn, you got into character, sat in the hot seat and fielded probing questions from the group. The interrogation could run from what your character had for breakfast to who would they try to save in a zombie apocalypse.

Apart from Shelta Lee, Yemi was my only other suspect now I had eliminated Muriel from my list. I suggested playing twenty questions as a fun way to get to know each other whilst we waited for our food. Dev and Yemi were less than enthusiastic about having to work for their supper, but everyone else was game, even Lawrence.

"I'll go first." Amy danced around in her seat. "Do we get points for the best answer?"

"No," I replied. "It's not a competition, just a bit of fun to get to know each other better."

"Shame, I thought the winner could pay for dessert. Anyway, let's start with you, Reverend Jess." Amy rested her elbows on the table and placed her chin on the back of her raised hands. "Talking about dessert, what's your favourite?"

Playing hardball straight out of the bat, eh?

"Depends on the weather," I replied. "If the sun is shining, cheesecake. If it's wet and dreary, apple crumble and custard. And you?"

"That's easy. Peach Melba. If the restaurant doesn't have it on the menu, I still ask them to make it. Any dessert chef worth his salt can rustle one up in no time."

Lawrence chimed in. "Provided they have peaches."

"There's always a tin at the back of the larder." Amy refolded her napkin and checked the position of her cutlery. I sat transfixed as she adjusted the placement of the fork, spoon and knife to be equal distance apart. The repetition of her movements was hypnotic.

A thud on the table made the same cutlery, and everyone else's, jump. Amy's arms shot under the table as she turned her head to glare at the culprit. "Yemi!"

"Tobias, I'm sorry. I can't do this anymore." Yemi pushed back his chair and stood up. His nostrils flared as he pointed down the table towards Amy. "She is psycho!"

Amy's eyes widened, her bottom lip trembled. "What have I done?"

"Don't pretend to be upset. We all know you are incapable of normal human emotions. You're a freak!" Yemi's anger spat out across the table.

Tobias raised his arm and tried to calm his friend down. "Mate, come on. I get it. You're a little cut up over today's events. Look. You can have a rest tomorrow, eh? We could hire a boat in the harbour. Go for a sail. The forecast for tomorrow is excellent. What d'ya say, eh?

Yemi panned our faces and dropped back down in his seat. "Yeah, maybe. Sounds good," he shrugged.

"Is that it?" Amy slammed her fist on the table. Her gesture appeared measured. Loud enough to demonstrate anger, but not too loud as to disturb the other diners. "You are going to let him get away with that?" she hissed.

"Cut him some slack, eh Amy? Say you're sorry, Yemi." Dev pleaded. His resigned expression made me think this was a recurring scene.

Not all one happy family then.

"She needs to apologise first." Yemi huffed as he reached for the breadbasket.

Amy folded her arms and kicked back in her chair, "I wasn't the one calling people psychopaths."

71

Yemi took a roll and ripped it in two. "No, you just, as always, wanted the world to dance to your tune. Peach melba! No one orders a peach melba. You always have to push. You don't give a thought to the overworked chef in the kitchen, who has lovingly crafted his dessert menu to present the finest local produce for your enjoyment. Peach, flaming, melba. You can't always have your own way." He stuffed one end of the roll in his mouth as if to stop any more words from coming out.

"Children. You are behaving like spoilt brats in front of our guests." Tobias's green eyes darted between the arguing couple. "And over dessert? We haven't even had our drinks yet."

Emily Sykes

F ood and drinks arrived a few minutes later. All discussion about desserts, or the idea
of twenty questions, abandoned for talk of who the best James Bond was. There
was a clear divide. The older members of the group rallied around Sean Connery, whilst
Dev and Amy plumped for Daniel Craig. Yemi stood alone with his choice of Timothy
Dalton.

"I worked with Daniel Craig back before his Bond days. He is a true professional." Tobias
chomped down on a thick slice of braised steak.

"Was that the Guy Ritchie film you were in?" I knew nothing about the film, not even its
name, but Mum had mentioned he had a part in one and I thought it was good to show
an interest.

"No. Some art-house piece. We played Russian antique dealers fleeing the USSR. I got
shot by the KGB within the first ten minutes of the film. I think it went straight to video,"
he laughed. "Or straight in the bin."

Lawrence took a sip of red wine. "Maybe it has a cult following on YouTube or something.
Have you checked?"

Tobias finished chewing. "To be honest, it's not my best work and I can't even remember
the title. I doubt it even gets a listing on Daniel's IMDb entry."

I was curious. "So, this was straight after drama school. It's good you didn't give up. You're one of the few from our class that's had any success."

"True. Your old boyfriend Hugo works in IT now, I heard. But once this airs, Jess, you can expect lots of work offers to flood in."

"I have no desire to court fame and fortune. *If* this gets to air, that'll be it. I promise you."

Tobias wiped a napkin across his mouth. His Cheshire cat grin emerged from beneath the stray red wine gravy. "Jessie, Jessie, Jessie. You still think the bishop will pull the plug, don't you? Time will tell. Amy isn't the only one here used to getting their own way."

*****

The usual suspects were present at the weekly parish council meeting in the church hall. Though they are mostly a well-turned-out bunch, news that the TV crew was coming had brought them all out in their Sunday best. Even Rosemary had succumbed to a touch of lipstick. The meeting itself made for dull entertainment.

On the agenda, the plight of the bell ringers, plans for the harvest festival service, and a brief discussion about going further afield for Christmas raffle prizes this year. The usual local turkey and festive food hampers would stay, but we all agreed we needed to source better gifts than a set of stainless-steel pans or a stepladder from Bits and Bobs.

After the meeting, I took charge of the washing up. The crew was quick to take advantage of the opportunity presented by all the leaders of my church community being gathered in one place. One by one, they took each of them into the main church for a quick piece to camera. Tom had been the first to volunteer and was now back in the hall's kitchen, helping me put the cups away.

"He's terribly attractive that Mr Dean. I understand you dated him years ago."

"Yes, for my sins." I stacked a pile of pale green saucers and passed them to Tom.

74

"Oh, we've all made mistakes in our youth. Funny how things come back to bite us in the rear when we least expect it." He hesitated over a cup and scratched the inner rim with his thumbnail. "I think you need to do this one again."

"Oops, thank you."

"Terribly sad business with poor Kat, eh, Reverend. I mean, she was away with the fairies, but no one deserves to go like that, do they?"

I shook my head and tutted. "No. Who would want to do something like that?"

"Don't you have any clues?" Tom used his entire face to wink his right eye. His gesture was so over the top, I fully expected a pantomime thigh slap to follow.

"I'm afraid this time, I don't have a scooby."

"I think it was someone at the seance. I mean, that turned dark *really* quickly." Tom grabbed a spare cloth from the counter and draped it over his head. "One of you is going to die!" he moaned in a ghoulish voice.

Then, in a single beat, his mood changed. He slid the makeshift hood off and looked down at the floor, twisting the towel in his hands. "Though it was lovely to see Avril and Verity get a visit, it was a bittersweet moment. I knew the Leybournes well. We grew up together."

Tom curled the dishcloth tight over his left hand. "I understand Avril thinks her father expected more of her. Roger Leybourne put a stern face to the world, but he was a good friend. And he adored his baby girls." He twisted his torso around enough to close the cupboard door, then rewound to lean back against the worktop. "Not everyone can be a teacher. The world needs hairdressers too."

A distant memory pinged across my mind like a silver ball in a game of bagatelle.

Mr Leybourne!

"Avril and Verity Leybourne? I am a complete idiot. Tom. Their father. He was the deputy head, wasn't he? And he married one of the other teachers. What was her name?"

"Emily." he sighed.

Back in the Seventies, the teachers and I were not on a first-term basis. "Tom, you know what I mean. What was her maiden name?"

"Oh, right. It's on the tip of my tongue. They married in '78. No, tell a lie. It was '77. She was positively glowing. What was her family name? It was such a long time ago... Same as the villain in Oliver Twist..."

Fagin?

"Yes, that's it. Bill Sykes."

"Miss Sykes. Oh my, I remember her so well. She was my final year teacher. Pretty. Kind. Emily Sykes. I never knew her first name. Emily suits her. When I was eleven, I thought she was the most beautiful woman in the world. She was like a flower."

Tom swallowed back a lump in his throat. "She was an angel." he sniffed. "You're determined to make me cry, Reverend. Good thing I've recorded my piece. These gorgeous eyes don't suit red and puffy."

A snivelling mess of a churchwarden fell in my direction. I propped him up as he sobbed onto my shoulder.

"It's okay to cry. They were good friends of yours."

"The best," he blubbered. "Do you really think their spirits were there in the room with us, Reverend?"

"I have to believe in the afterlife. It's part of the job."

"There's a comfort in that, isn't there? So many of my friends and family have passed. I don't know what I'd do if Ernest goes before me."

"I'm not going anywhere, you're soppier than that dishcloth you're holding." Ernest magically appeared beside us. "Reverend, I'll take it from here. He's been in a strange mood lately. Come on Tom, you old fool. Let's go home."

Though he remained upbeat in front of Tom, Ernest wore a sombre smile as he guided his partner out of the kitchen. When he reached the door, he looked back and mouthed "I've got him."

One by one, the rest of the PCC filmed their big moment and made their way home. Only Phil and Barbara hung around to travel down to the Cat and Fiddle with their guests.

Phil was stacking the hall chairs in the storage room. I grabbed a stray and caught him as he was about to close the door. "Room for one more?"

"How did I miss that? Thanks, Vicar."

I hadn't had a lot of time to talk to Phil, my trusty verger, over the past few months. Their wedding in June and then running the pub during the peak of the summer tourist season had kept him busy and away from the church.

"It'll be good to see the tourists heading home. There are lots of odd jobs for you to do here. Should keep you busy all winter."

Phil lifted the last chair to the top of the rickety wooden tower. "That's the way of things. No rest for the wicked."

"Phil Vickers, there is nothing wicked about you." Barbara's voice echoed across the cavernous wooden building.

"Well, Mrs Vickers, we'll see about that when we get home," he joked.

Barbara giggled. It was beautiful to see their playful side.

"I think we can lock up here and go through to the church," I suggested.

"Vicar, there's something Barbara and I have been meaning to tell you." Phil waved for his wife to walk over. "You see. I'm sure it's just a coincidence, but there was something very fishy about the behaviour of some of the film crew that night."

"What night?"

"The night Kat Pringle was murdered."

"How fishy?" I whispered.

"Well," Phil checked for eavesdroppers, "the cameraman, Yemi? He came down as I was closing up and asked for a key. He said he couldn't sleep and was going to go for a ride."

"Okay." This was interesting and lifted Yemi right to the top of my suspect list. "Did you see when he got back?"

Phil shook his head. "No, but 'e was there for breakfast at seven."

"You said 'some'. Were any of the others acting strange?"

Barbara snuggled into our impromptu huddle. "Not so much about that night, but the young girl goes jogging along the Wesberrey Road every morning. She jumps on the milk round and then runs back along the coastal path."

The 'milk round' is the name locals give to a farmer's cart that circles the island every morning delivering milk, eggs, and other farm goods. Traditionally, people have always cadged a free ride as it goes on its rounds.

"What time does it pass the pub?"

"We usually get our delivery before six, anytime after half five, unless the cows have got out onto the road or something." Phil straightened himself up. We had all arched over to talk, and his back was giving out. "Oh, that's better. Where was I? Ah, yes. She asked about places to run when she checked in. You 'ave to admire her dedication. She was up and out before breakfast again this morning."

"And she came back in time for breakfast?"

"I'm pretty sure she did, but I couldn't say for certain. We are very busy. I don't remember her not being there." Barbara cupped her hand over her mouth. "Unlike your ex-boyfriend. He was very late. The others had cleaned their plates and were on their coffee when he arrived. You couldn't miss him. He was boasting about the amazing night he'd had."

"Men like that have no class. Film star or not, you don't besmirch a lady's reputation like that over a plate of bacon and eggs. And certainly not two."

I struggled to follow Phil's meaning. "Two plates of bacon and eggs?"

"No. Two ladies!" My tight-lipped verger was reluctant to name names, but his wife was less discreet.

"The Leybournes. Avril and Verity. I shudder to think what they got up to on my clean sheets."

Crumpets

I'm not sure I would have wanted to cavort with an ageing film star in a room above where my dead parents had manifested earlier that evening, but each to their own. Nor would I be particularly in favour of a threesome with my sister, but I'm not a twin.

I was curious though about when they departed and if they had witnessed Yemi leaving or coming back. As Tobias had granted the crew a day off, following Yemi and Amy's tiff at the restaurant, I finally would have some free time to get out there and start sleuthing.

As Thursday morning slid through the cracks in my bedroom curtains, I took out a notepad and made a list of people I needed to speak to that day. The first item to check off was a visit to Market Square. Shelta may still be staying with the Needhams, so I needed to get there quickly. If she had already left for the mainland, then I had a ferry to catch. But not before I caught up with the Leybourne twins.

"Nice of you to pop in, Reverend. Are you here for the vigil?" Avril tidied the dog-eared magazines on the waiting area's coffee table.

"What vigil?"

Verity was refilling the sapphire water sanitiser at her workstation. "For Kat Pringle. God rest her soul. The stallholders are taking a minute's silence at eleven o'clock." She plopped some black combs into the container.

"That's a lovely gesture. I will try to attend."

"So Vicar," Avril slid behind the reception desk and flipped open a large pink appointment diary. "When shall I book you in?"

"Oh, right. I actually didn't come in to make an appointment, but I suppose whilst I'm here." I took out my phone and after a bit of toing and froing, we settled on a date for a much needed cut and blow-dry.

Avril leant over the table and picked at my hair. "I put you in for a colour as well. Your roots will be shocking by then." She scribbled the date and time on a card and handed it to me. "So, what did you come in for?"

"Er, I was wondering if you saw Yemi, the cameraman with Tobias Dean, coming or going from the pub on Tuesday night?"

The two sisters looked furtively at each other. Verity came across and nudged Avril out of the way so that she could get to the petty cash box. "I need to pop to D and V before we open. Your sister has started doing spiced pumpkin lattes. Have you tried them? I'll get you one. They are delicious."

"Verity. Thank you, but please can you wait just a minute? I know you were with Tobias that night." Avril fell into the receptionist's chair. Verity steadied herself on the back of the same chair. "I'm not here to judge. Honest. I want to help find Kat's killer and, well, she had an affair with Yemi years ago. That makes him a prime suspect, you see?"

"Vicar, just so you know, we don't normally do that sort of thing. But he's Tobias Dean. I mean, you would, wouldn't you?"

And I did. Though he had more hair on his head back then.

I smiled.

"No comment. He who is without sin cast the first stone and all that. Did you see him?"

Verity shook her head.

Avril took a breath. "No," she answered. "But I saw someone else. I was looking out the window. I'm not sure of the exact time, but it was well after midnight."

"Do you know who it was?"

"It was too dark, and they had a hood up. And they wore some kind of neon jacket like the ones builders wear. They went into the bakery."

Must be Shelta Lee!

*****

Next stop, the Needhams. The couple were busy with their final preparations for a full day of trading. As before, the smell of fresh bread was intoxicating. They were good people, and I prayed in my heart that their niece was innocent. The evidence, so far, looked pretty damning.

Shelta had a motive, was clearly prone to violent outbursts, and was likely out on the night of Kat Pringle's murder. Both she and Kat were vehemently against any form of mediation after their fight, and she still looked angry at the seance. Yet, she was suddenly prepared to kiss and make up when Amy called her.

Amy can be very persuasive and some people will do anything if it means they will appear on television, but it would be even easier to agree to something you know will never happen.

"Good morning, Reverend." John Needham dusted flour from his hands and stretched across to shake mine. "Everything alright with the wheatsheaf?"

"Oh, yes. Thank you. It arrived in one piece, fortunately, and is now in pride of place on the church altar."

"That's good news, eh, my dear?"

Deborah Needham chortled in response. "Oh, good news indeed, my love. Not sure we could have made another before the service tomorrow. We're rushed off our feet, aren't we, love?"

"Yes, we are my dear, rushed off our feet."

"Actually, I was hoping to talk to your niece, Shelta? I thought I could offer her some solace at this difficult time."

"What difficult time would that be now, Reverend?" Deborah fussed over some iced buns in a wooden box tray on the counter.

"The death of Kat Pringle. Shelta knew her. There was a slight fracas by Kat's stall earlier that day. I thought Shelta might need some words of comfort this morning after the police interviewed her."

"Oh, is that why that man with the moustache was here yesterday?" Deborah had moved her attention onto some cinnamon rolls.

"Yes, that was Inspector Lovington."

"Well, he was very complimentary about my scones. Wasn't he, my love?"

"Oh, that he was, my dear. Very complimentary. Has to be said, that batch had a very good rise on them."

"They did indeed, my love. Now, Vicar, you want to see our Shelta?"

"Yes, Mrs Needham. Is she upstairs?"

"Oh no, Vicar. She went home when the gentleman left. Took some crumpets with her. Shelta loves my crumpets, doesn't she, my love?"

"Shelta loves her crumpets, my dear, that she does."

*****

I decided to hang around for the vigil and catch the next ferry over. As well as learning about Shelta's love for crumpets, I also got her address. As Pam had told me earlier, Shelta Lee lived in a hamlet to the west of Oysterhaven in the village of Elton.

Whilst enjoying an oat milk latte at Rosie's cafe, a quick Wikipedia search informed me that the hamlet was originally an Anglo-Saxon settlement and means the place of the eels. Eel Creek still runs through it into the sea beyond, though the snake-like fish and the men and women who made a living catching them are long gone.

"What are you reading there, Vicar?" Stanley Matthews plonked his ample frame on the chair beside me.

"Would you believe the history of Elton? I don't think I have ever been there."

"Well, you'd have no cause to, would you? Just a bunch of gypsies and new age travellers there now. I doubt many are buying what you have to offer." He pointed a stubby finger at my dog collar.

"Used to visit with my dad back in the day. He loved him some jellied eels for tea. How times change, eh? Now we have smashed avocado on toast, and everything's covered in rocket. That was a weed when I was a kid. Audrey loves the stuff. And I hear tripe's coming back in fashion. I'll take a pass on that. Sheep stomach?" he shuddered. "No way."

"So, what's your poison?" I asked.

"Oh, nothing fancy. Just a hot Americano with extra coffee and steamed almond milk with a shot of vanilla."

I could feel the irony twitching my lips into a smirk. "Sounds wonderful."

Stanley took a long, satisfying sip from his mug. "So why are you going to Elton?"

"To see Shelta Lee."

"Really? On church business, or are you sniffing around for clues?" His coffee breath made a beeline for my nostrils.

I would be bouncing off the ceiling if I drank that.

"I can't lie to you, Stan. It's a bit of both."

"I knew it. I was saying to Audrey last night, it's only a matter of time before the vicar gets Ms Lee in her sights. I saw her, of course."

I choked on my latte. "You saw her? When?"

Stanley sat back in his chair. A smug snort followed. He pursed his lips into a wry smile. "That night, well morning I should say, about two a.m. when I put out the bins. I had just finished catching up on the *Match of the Day* highlights on BBC iPlayer. I watch the footie when Audrey goes to bed. She's not a fan."

"And what did you see?"

"Shelta Lee. No mistake. She's been visiting her aunt and uncle since she was a child. Was hard to miss her, she had on a Hi-vis jacket. Her hood was up, but I knew it was her. I guess she'd been for a ride. She was walking beside her bike. Very sensible, the cobbles are a nightmare round the square, would be way too dangerous to cycle in the dark."

"So, you saw Shelta returning home at two in the morning?"

"That's right, Vicar. Now, doesn't that seem a tad suspicious to you?"

It most certainly did.

The Vigil

All the shops around the square closed out of respect and, as eleven o'clock approached, stallholders and their patrons ceased trading and united in silence around Kat's former stall.

As the blue-faced clock on the Guildhall tower struck the hour, a lone bell from St. Bridget's marked out eleven chimes across the stillness.

There were no words, no eulogy. Simply a reverential bowing of heads and personal contemplation. I took the time to send a few words up to the Big Guy. Asking for the people gathered to find peace in their loss.

The minute up, the general hubbub of market life returned once more.

I finished my prayer and headed towards the ferry. Yemi and Dev stood outside the Cat and Fiddle, dismantling their equipment.

"Hi guys, I thought you had a day off?"

"Make that an afternoon," grumbled Yemi into his camera bag.

"Tobias found out about the vigil and thought it was too good to miss." Dev picked at a leaf that had stuck itself to his microphone's fluffy boom cover. "Got a lie in though, so not all bad."

"So, do you have any plans for your afternoon off? The forecast is good, given the time of year."

"Tobias said something about hiring a boat or something. A fishing trip, maybe. He thinks it will help bond us together."

Yemi muttered something under his breath that I couldn't make out.

"Are you sure being enclosed in a small space together out at sea is a wise idea, given the tensions yesterday?"

Zipping up his black canvas bag, Yemi raised himself up to his full height and threw the holdall over his shoulder. "What tensions?" he sneered. "Didn't you know, Reverend Ward, we're just one big happy family."

Dev patted his colleague on the back, and they walked back into the pub. As they reached the door, Dev turned back. "Enjoy the respite, Reverend. We'll be back hungry for more tomorrow."

*****

I had parked Cilla next to the ferry. On market day, it's often hard to find a space in the square itself. I had a few minutes to wait until the ferry docked. I welcomed the opportunity to sit back on the harbour wall and people-watch. Or should I say cat watch?

The local feral cats usually mill around the harbour during the day, picking up morsels of food from the fishing boats or tourists. Children often arrive armed with tasty treats for their favourite strays. Cats on Wesberrey are rarely skinny.

Over the past nine months, I had gotten to know some of their distinct personalities. There were obvious leaders and followers. Outsiders circled around the main packs, waiting their turn. Generations of independent felines living by their rules on the fringe of human society.

Was human society so different, though? Most of us find a way to fit in, negotiate the best survival terms we can through the networks we operate in. We develop mutually beneficial relationships with family, friends, colleagues and associates, even strangers who bestow random acts of kindness that make our lives more manageable. But society also forces some of us to operate on the edge. Waiting for an opening, or stalking our prey. For those on the outside, normal rules don't apply.

Kat Pringle was on the margins. Did that make her the victim of another's predator goals?

As I observed harbour life, the midday sun warmed my back. Soon, autumn would bring clouds to mask her healing rays. It was a beautiful day to be taking a trip across the bay. Whatever secrets lay ahead of me in Elton.

The ferry crossing was smooth, if busy. Once disembarked, I walked alongside Cilla for a few hundred yards to avoid accidentally running over a school party that had been on a trip from the mainland. *Excited, tired children are so unpredictable!*

The journey to Elton forced me to go through the main roads of Oysterhaven. Traffic was heavy. It was trips like this that made me appreciate the slow equine pace of life on Wesberrey. Finally, the wide roads and pavements became a narrow lane that crossed an ancient stone bridge. On the other side sat the village of Elton. Just a few minutes outside of town and a world apart.

To my left, marshland. To my right, static caravans. Rows upon rows of metal homes on cement blocks laid out across the horizon. Lines strung between trailers waved today's laundry in the breeze. At the far end stood a traveller park, whose matching houses had wheels and dogs tethered on long chains.

Closer to the centre, Victorian worker's cottages painted in a rainbow of colours lined the single road that merged into the medieval high street. Here, houses slanted to their sides. The original builders presumably made their painted front doors for hobbits. Cute, but not suitable for modern inhabitants. At the central junction stood a wattle and daub, beamed structure. The faded wooden sign outside announced this was the 'Olde Court Hall' built circa 1450.

The High Street continued down a slight incline, and on a corner, nestled between a pharmacy and a Chinese takeaway, was Shelta's shop. I parked around the bend and

VESTRY VICE

walked back. Fairy lights and purple bunting hung across the bay window. In white stencils in the centre of the window, read the words 'The Howlet's Wing.'

What a curious name?

The part-glazed purple gloss door bore the same white stencils. I turned the knob and stepped down across the threshold. A small brass bell announced my visit.

To the rear of the shop stood a black-based glass cabinet that acted as a customer desk and till point. Wooden shelving units lined the other two walls. Each one contained glass vials and mason jars of coloured liquids and powders. In the centre, a low-level unit covered in velvet, was baskets of polished stones, bound sprigs of sage and small gossamer bags filled with basil and bay leaves. Lit candles balanced on the edge of every free surface. And from the beams of the ceiling hung sprigs of herbs, dried lavender, crystals, and small cloth effigies with tiny red fabric hearts sewn on their chests.

Voodoo dolls?

I inspected the closest shelf. The labels on the vials professed to contain 'Dragon's Blood' ink.

"Dragon's Blood!"

"Good afternoon, Reverend. Don't worry. I promise the dragons survived the procedure." Shelta emerged from a beaded curtain in the back wall.

"So, it's not real?"

Jess? Dragons. Of course, it's not real!

"It's a plant-based dye. From the leaves of the tree." Shelta reached across to pull out a jar containing a chicken's foot. "Unfortunately, the chicken didn't make it."

"Why the skull and crossbones on some labels? Are they poisonous?"

"No, just the logo of my hoodoo line."

Of course.

"Are they real coffin nails?"

Shelta nodded.

"And did you really get that soil from a graveyard?"

"I always leave a little gift behind to say thank you."

Oh, that's alright then.

I swallowed my desire to scream. Polite conversation, that's what the British do best. Small talk. The weather and so on.

"The shop's name. I'm curious. What's a howlet's wing?"

"Macbeth." Shelta rummaged through a cardholder on the glass desk. "The witches chant. Lizard's leg and howlet's wing." She waved her tattooed hand in my general direction. "You know the one. Double, double toil and trouble; fire burn and cauldron bubble. All that jazz."

"Ah, right. Brilliant." Her explanation didn't make me feel any better. "What are you looking for?"

"I have some saint's prayer cards you might be interested in. What about St. Jude, the patron saint of lost causes and hopeless cases?"

"Not really my thing. Prayers to saints are the other guys."

Shelta's black lips parted to reveal dazzling white teeth.

No fangs. Phew!

"Oh, you're Protestant. Of course, silly me. One of those fire and brimstone types?"

"No, I like to think that I am very open-minded."

Really? You just thought she was a vampire!

"Hmm, like your aunts?" Shelta pulled out two folding chairs from behind the desk and flipped them open. "Please sit yourself down. I think you'll find we have a lot in common."

The Howlet's Wing

"You're looking pastier than usual, Reverend Ward. Would you like some liquorice tea?"

"Er, no. Thank you. I grabbed a macchiato at the Whistle Stop Cafe." *Jess, get a grip on yourself. Why are you lying?*

"Really? Does your sister know you frequent other coffee shops?"

Shelta crossed one black fishnet leg over the knee of the other. Her laced edged skirt split in two and the loosened fabric slid down either side of the chair, revealing her hi-laced black Dr Martens. She looked like a grungy Elvira if you replaced the enhanced cleavage with a Nirvana top.

"Oh, you know Rosie?"

"Of course, I am always at my aunt's and uncle's. Families, right. It's important to look after the older members. Cherish their anecdotes and their wisdom."

"How are you related?" *I thought gypsies married from within the community.*

"Ah, that would be through my grandmother. She and Aunt Debbie left the travelling life behind in the mid-sixties. They ran away to find fame and fortune, but with no education nor a penny to their name, they ended up married to two gorgers. They settled here because they wanted to keep the old ways alive. That's how they met your aunts. Small world, eh, Reverend?"

"Yes, yes, it is."

"But that's not why you came to see me, is it?" Shelta flicked a speck of powder off her knee.

"No. Actually, I came to offer you an opportunity to talk about Kat Pringle. I know you had your disagreements, but her death must have come as a shock."

Shelta laughed. "I thought confessionals were for Catholics? You said you are the other lot, right?"

"I'm not suggesting you killed Kat!"

Unless you did, of course.

"I see. So, it wasn't you who told Inspector Lovington to put me at the top of his list of suspects."

How would she know that?

"I had to tell him about your brawl at the market."

She uncrossed her legs and planted the elevated foot firmly on the floor. "Oh, did you now?"

I twitched the corners of my mouth into what I hoped was an endearing smile.

"I suppose it's too late to accept that offer of tea? I am feeling a little thirsty since you mentioned it."

Shelta flashed her tombstone grin. "Of course not. If you prefer, I have some Earl Grey at the back of the cupboard." I shook my head. "Wise decision. Goodness knows how long that's been there. Er, you're not going to make a run for it, are you? Seems a shame to come all this way and not get the answers you seek."

She swished back behind the curtain. I followed. To offer to help, not to spy.

The kitchen was little more than a pantry with a stainless-steel sink, an overhead cupboard, and an electric kettle. To my right was another door. It stood ajar enough for me to see a toilet. There was only room for one inside, so I loitered in the doorway.

"I'm sorry, but I think we got off on the wrong foot."

"Really? And what makes you think that?" She sliced through the cardboard lid of a box of commercial tea and plonked a tea bag into two waiting cups.

"You drink the supermarket's finest." I gasped, probably a tad too surprised, given the domestic situation.

"Why did you think I was brewing a batch in my cauldron?" She giggled. "You god-fearing types are all the same. I had hoped with your pedigree I could expect you to... never mind. These need to stand for a few minutes. Let's carry them back next door."

"Pedigree? I'm not a dog!"

"I could make some cutting remark about coming from a long line of bitches, but that would be an insult to your ancestors." Shelta adjusted her skirt as she sat. "So, fire away. I know you have a lot of questions."

I have confronted murderers before, but now I realised I had no evidence of any kind to prove the woman in front of me knew anything about Kat Pringle's death.

"Where were you after the seance?"

"Hmm, good opener. I was at Kat Pringle's house."

Stay calm, Jess. Think about what you want to ask next.

"And did you go there straight after you left the pub? Did you go with Kat?"

"That's two questions. No and no."

"So where did you go first, then?"

"I escorted my elderly relatives home, like a good great-niece. Family comes first, always."

"And then?"

"At this rate, we're going to be here all evening. Look, let me put you out of your misery."

"Okay." I stretched across to the counter to get my mug. A wave of aniseed assaulted my nostrils. "That's stronger than I expected."

"Take a sip. It's great for stomach ailments." Shelta leant back and folded her arms across Kurt Cobain's face. Her eyebrows arched as I sipped her shop-bought brew. "Well?"

I smacked my lips. "It's delicious."

"Really? I can get you something else if you don't like it."

"No, honestly. It's very nice. So, you went back to the bakery. Then what happened?"

"I took my bicycle and rode out to Travellers Bay."

"To see Kat Pringle?"

"To apologise. I wanted to do it at the pub, but ooh, that stupid cow just makes me see red."

"What was it about Kat Pringle that irked you so much? She seemed lovely to me. Maybe a tad melancholy? Wistful, but harmless."

This tea really is lovely.

"All an act. She had everyone fooled."

"What did she do?"

"She stole my business."

I looked around the shop. *What did Kat rob? Some newts' eyes or boomslang shavings?*

"Surely there's room for healthy competition. She has the lavender corn dollies and you have the lizard's claw?"

"Don't tell me you bought all that pink fluffy unicorn nonsense. She wanted the dark arts. I used to run closed workshops right here in the shop. You know, energy work, witch bottles, tarot, etc. She came along every week. Keen as mustard."

"So, you got to know her very well. When was this?"

"About two years ago. She wanted me to teach her how to perform love spells. I don't do anything that controls another's will. I could earn a fortune that way, but I sleep soundly at night knowing I am helping people attract good things into their life or banishing problems. No harm, no foul."

"Do many people ask for love spells?" I cast my eyes up at the voodoo dolls hanging above me.

"Yes, and hexes. People love to curse each other."

"So, you didn't teach her that stuff?"

"No, but the internet has everything on there if you know where to look."

"Do you know why she wanted all this?"

"Yeah, to steal my business, I told you. I found out that she took my workshop notes and ran her own classes using my lesson plans. She shared spells and healing recipes handed down to me through generations of my line. Miss Kat Rainbow Fairy Dust Pringle even cloned my website. I mean image for image. Word for word."

"That's outrageous."

"Really? You think?" Shelta huffed and took a giant gulp of liquorice tea. I wasn't sure, in the half-light of the shop, but she looked like she was crying.

"That explains your outburst at the stall. But murder?"

"You don't get it, do you? I didn't kill her! No harm, no foul, remember?"

No Harm, No Foul

"It was late for a bike ride, especially as the lights are few along the Wesberrey Road," Shelta explained, "but I have been cycling around the island since I was a kid. And that road's a great big circle. It's hard to get lost."

"Well, I'm never sure where the turning is for Travellers Bay in the daylight. So how do you do it in the dark?"

"Like I said, I know the roads. I also trust in my instincts. I set my intentions, and they never fail to guide me to my destination."

"You have your own internal sat-nav," I joked. Anything to ease the tension.

"Don't we all? If what I hear is correct, Reverend Ward, daughter of the Sisters Bailey, you're plugged into the mother ship through a direct line."

"Still, you're very brave to venture out alone at night in this day and age."

"What with murderers on the loose? Maybe you're right." Shelta slapped her thigh with her free hand and moved forward in her chair. "Though, if I'm the killer, I really have nothing to fear."

"But you're not. You said."

"Hmm." Shelta tipped up her mug to empty the dregs of her tea into a potted plant on the counter. "Always share what you have. I have more than enough."

"So, I take it Kat was alive when you got there?"

"Yep. She said she knew I was coming." Shelta laughed. "Like really? No way she knew. She was already in her nightdress. Who changes for bed if they're expecting company?"

"So, what time did you get there?" I swirled the last of my tea around my cup and reached over to empty it into the pot. *When in Rome...*

Shelta smirked.

"I would say just after midnight. Kat invited me in. We talked. She got defensive. She bare-faced lied to me. But there were no fisticuffs this time. I'm a forgiving soul. I offered her the chance to join forces. If you can't beat them, join them, eh?" Shelta was as earnest as a used car salesman. "I told her she could set up a new site offering the pink, fluffy love spells or hexes for embittered exes. And I would teach her all she needed to know, as long as she stopped doing my work."

"What happened to no harm, no foul?"

My nose twitched. I flexed my nostrils to appease the embryonic sneeze tickling my nasal cavity. I had a sudden urge to stretch.

"Er, I'm sorry. Do you mind if I move around a bit?"

Shelta granted my request with a majestic wave of her spidery wrist.

"Knock yourself out."

My witchy host extended out her arms and legs to their fullest and yawned. I wanted to copy her. *Yawns are so contagious.* But I stifled the feeling before it set itself free.

"By showing Kat what to do, I release responsibility," she continued. "I'm not liable for the consequences. I am merely the teacher. No one can hold me accountable for how my pupils use their knowledge. Is a chemistry teacher guilty if their student uses what they taught them to make a bomb?"

This gypsy-gorger, hybrid pagan purveyor of potions, had such a powerful aura. An elegant, no-nonsense, down-to-earth grandeur. Every word she spoke floated on the air, carried by the musky incense she burned on the table. It was hypnotic and disturbing.

Enigmatic, that's the word. The more she spoke, the less I believed she was capable of murder, and yet there was something that unnerved me.

"So, did you show her a spell on Tuesday night?"

She nodded. "Nothing binding, just a 'Come to me' spell. Very basic stuff. Just a special blend of herbs and intention."

"No bloodletting under a full moon, then?" I smiled, picking up an ornate silver bookmark from a shelf near the window display.

"Not for this one." Shelta giggled. "You really know very little about your heritage."

"I didn't even know I had a heritage a year ago. Aunt Cindy promised that Mystic Muriel would help enlighten me, but that didn't turn out too great, did it?"

"Muriel is a rare find. Her knowledge is limited, but when it comes to mediumship, she's your woman." Shelta stood up and joined me in my walk around the shop.

"You know, I'd be happy to teach you."

"Thank you. I'll bear that in mind. I've taken up too much of your time already." I picked up my stuff and backed slowly towards the entrance. "It'll be dark soon."

"Well, you know where I am now. And as you can see, I'm not rushed off my feet." Shelta pressed past me to open the door. I hadn't noticed before how she smelt of moss. She reminded me of a walk in the forest after a thunderstorm. It was bizarre. I never usually notice odours unless they are bad. The aroma that now caressed my nostrils was earthy and sweet.

Lavender and sea salt?

"Just one last question before I go. What time did you leave Kat's house?"

"Would have been a little after one o'clock. I didn't stay long."

"And did you see anyone else on your way back?"

"You said that was your last question." Shelta opened the door.

The chilly evening air blew in from the street. The flavours of the Chinese restaurant rode shotgun.

Sesame seed oil, ginger, oyster sauce and fried rice.

Shelta and I sniffed in tandem. She grinned. "Smells delicious. Think I might get a takeaway for dinner. As to your question. Did I see anybody? To be honest, I'm not sure. It was dark. Nothing stood out as being weird or anything."

I stepped outside. I could sense Shelta was lingering in the doorway behind me. "One more thing. When you did the 'Come to Me' spell with Kat, did you just walk through the motions, or do it for real?"

"Ah, there's the detective. I wondered when she'd show up. We did it for real, but don't ask me who she summoned because I didn't ask. It was none of my business."

*****

A gazillion thoughts danced around my mind on the drive back through Oysterhaven. Who was Kat trying to enchant? Could I really trust my intuition with Shelta, or had she charmed me with one of her spells? Was Kat Pringle actually a sneaky, underhand thief playing a gangster in the pagan world? *What does that even mean?*

I slowed down on the approach to the roundabout at the junction of the road to the ferry and the main town centre. The roads were heavy with workers eager to get home. Idling cars and lorries pumped their exhausts into the air. The fumes swam in and out of my helmet. Filling my nose, clawing at my throat.

The traffic lights turned green, but I couldn't focus on the road ahead. Frustrated motorists sounded their horns. The honk, honk, honk echoed off the office buildings around me.

My eyelids felt heavy.

The world went dark.

Smells Like Teen Spirit

"*Can I interest you in a poppet, deary? Or maybe some lucky heather? Read your palm for a fiver.*" *An old lady thrust a few twigs of heather wrapped in tin foil into my hand.*

"*I'm not buying.*" *I stumbled back.* "*Get away from me, you old crone.*"

"*Now that's not very polite, deary. Let me see your future. What does your heart desire?*"

I pushed her away. "*Nothing. Leave me alone. Please, somebody, help me!*"

"Can you tell me your name?"

Who's there?

"Reverend, can you tell me your name?"

"Jess. Jess Ward"

"Well, Jess Ward. You had a bit of a turn. But it doesn't look like you've broken anything."

A young man in a green jumpsuit appeared at my side. There was something covering my nose and mouth. I tried to pull it off.

"We've put an oxygen mask on you. You went an interesting shade of blue." He directed his attention to someone or something behind me. "I think we have her back now. If I had to name the colour, I'd say something like airforce blue."

Back now? Airforce blue?

An upside-down female in a matching jumpsuit moved into my line of sight.

"Hmm, blue grey like the uniform? I'll give you that one. Just relax, Reverend Ward. You had us all worried there for a second. Now, Jess, are you on any medication?"

I shook my head.

"When did you last eat?" The woman in green lifted my right eyelid. A bright light followed. Then she did the same on the left.

"Breakfast? Maybe?"

"We need to take your blood pressure. Okay?"

"Er, okay."

I must have fainted!

The male paramedic wrapped my arm with an inflatable strap. It squeezed my flesh like a boa constrictor. "We'll take you to the hospital in a few minutes. It's not far."

The ground was hard and cold. I tried to sit up.

"Hold your horses, young lady. Let me help you." The female paramedic put her arms through mine and lifted me up onto the curb. "There, that's better. Dan, pass me a blanket."

A short time later, my green rescuers strapped me to a gurney. 'Dan' hung with me in the back of the ambulance whilst his partner drove. Full sirens blaring and lights flashing.

"Do you think they will keep me in overnight? I feel fine now."

Dan checked his watch. "Hopefully, they will let you out this evening. All your vitals are fine now. They will want to do a few tests. Depends on how busy they are in A&E, but my monies on you going home tonight. Do you have a number to call someone to come and get you? If not, we can arrange a taxi?"

"No, I should be fine. Thank you."

*****

And I was.

Fine, that is.

Confused? Totally. Embarrassed? Hugely.

But physically, I was fine. Only a few bruises from when I collapsed, and Cilla fell with me.

"It could have been much worse. You're very lucky." Mum dragged a stool across her living room floor and placed my feet upon it.

"Mum, I told you. I can go back to the vicarage. You didn't need to bring me here."

Lawrence patted my hand. "Jess, your mother knows best. I know mine always does. You need to have complete rest."

Both of them had been clucking around me since they arrived at the hospital.

"But I need to prepare for Bishop Marshall's visit tomorrow. He's coming to the assembly." I wriggled to the edge of Mum's new mustard sofa. Its deep velvet cushions kept sucking me back in.

Even the furniture is against me!

"Jess, sit down. The doctors said you experienced a vasovagal syncope. The underlying cause was most likely anxiety related. Something triggered that response." Lawrence's ability to make a quick Google search sound like he studied the subject as his PhD thesis always amazed me. "It's not the first time you have fainted, is it? You still haven't told us what you were doing in Oysterhaven."

There was no bluffing my way out of this. Sandwiched between a headteacher and a grandmother, they would detect a lie a mile off.

"I was visiting Shelta Lee in Elton," I mumbled.

"Jessamy Ward! You went to the Howlet's Wing! Are you insane?" Mum's frustration ricocheted around her lounge. It landed in my heart as she paced before me, muttering to herself.

"She's put a spell on you. I know it. I will need Pam and Cindy. We'll need to break it. Harvest moon tonight. No time to waste. If only I knew what work she'd done. What would she have used? How?"

Mum paused as her breath caught up with her thoughts.

"Did she offer you a drink?"

I squirmed. "Liquorice tea?"

Lawrence caressed the back of my neck. "Beverley, you don't think she poisoned her?"

Hearing my boyfriend call my mother by her first name jarred a little. *Well, he can't call her Mum... yet.*

"Not intending to hurt her, no. But..." Mum rubbed her eyes as she processed the information.

No harm, no foul.

"Mum, I'm not an idiot. I followed Shelta to the kitchen and watched her make it. She used a supermarket's own brand tea bag, straight from a fresh box. It was tea."

"Did she do anything strange?"

"She poured the bottom of her cup into a plant pot."

"Did you copy her?"

I examined the parquet pattern on the floor and lifted my head up and down.

"Good."

I didn't expect that response.

"It's not a hex. It's a 'High sense' spell." Mum's furrowed brow softened like ripples in a still bucket. "Brilliant work, really. I need to check with my sisters about potential side effects. Those kinds of spells are so old school. Intention is key. She had to bond with you. Your mirroring her behaviour created a connection."

"I don't understand. There was no chanting. No calling on the spirits of the four winds or anything like that."

Mum collapsed into a matching armchair. "You have watched way too much TV." She kicked off her shoes. "Right, let me explain. When you pray, do you always say things out loud?"

"Of course not."

"Exactly, the power comes from the words you say in your heart. Head. Whatever. Basically, Shelta is trying to help you find Kat's killer. I imagine she has good olfactory skills herself and she wants to heighten your senses so you can pick up on more earthly clues. You can also share what you know or skills you possess."

Mum breathed out heavily. "You just had a bit of an overreaction. It will wear off in a few days."

I glanced at Lawrence. He knew my question before I'd even asked. "Olfactory means relating to your sense of smell."

"Oh, yes. Of course. I knew that."

I didn't.

"Does that mean I can go home now?"

"Yes, I suppose it's okay." She plumped up the cushion behind her and sniffed. "Just stay away from garlic."

"Haha, very funny. When is the bus due?

Mum pointed at the grandmother clock resting on the floor against the wall. "You have about ten minutes."

I jumped up and gave her an enormous hug. "Love you."

As always, Mum brushed off my physical display of affection.

I sighed. "Do you want Lawrence to put up that clock on the wall before we leave?"

"I'm not sure where I want it yet. It was your father's. He inherited it from his grandfather,"

"I know, Mum. I used to live with you, remember? I grew up with it chiming the quarter-hour.""Oh, it doesn't do that anymore." She laughed. "I'm not sure it goes with my new sofa."

"Mum, chuck it away if you want to. Or donate it to the Christmas bazaar. Time to move on. We don't need to hold on to the past."

Her glassy eyes were close to breaking. "Get on, you two. It's an hour till the next ride."

*****

"You miss her, don't you?" Lawrence wrapped his arms around my shoulders.

"She needed her own space. And Mum deserves her freedom. All her adult life, she has looked after us and then Zuzu's girls as well. It's time we all learned to stand on our own two feet."

I snuggled against his chest. The evening had a frosty edge. The full moon hung like a gold bauble in the dark sky. Tonight's autumnal equinox marked the end of summer and heralded in both death and rebirth. We have gathered in the harvest. Now we need to say thank you for God's grace and nature's bounty.

"Jess, will you be okay with the assembly tomorrow? I can always lead the prayers if you're not up to it. You were in the hospital a few hours ago. Everyone would understand."

"Lawrence, I promise you, I'm okay." I stroked his jaw but instantly regretted agitating the resting droplets of cologne on his nine o'clock shadow. "Though you could take it a little easier on the aftershave, it's peeling the corneas off my eyeballs."

"What I don't understand. And I'm saying this as a man that, truth be told, doesn't understand any of this. Why would anyone want you to smell more intensely?"

"I think Shelta intuitively knows that smell is the key. Lavender and sea salt. There's a clue there somewhere."

Lawrence pulled back and lifted my chin. "Yes, but why didn't she just tell you to look more closely at the lavender and salt clues? That's what a normal person would do."

"Babe, haven't you met my family?" I wriggled free to reinforce what I was about to say. "These witchy types are anything but normal. Why would they just straight-up tell someone something when they can wrap it up in riddles and satin bows and send it by carrier pigeon?"

"Enigmatic."

"Yes, enigmatic. That's the word. That's exactly the right word. Though frustrating, annoying and just plain stupid, come very close."

"So, how do you plan to use your new bloodhound trick?"

"I don't. This stuff always leads me down a rabbit hole. I am going to get some real clues. I haven't eliminated Shelta from my list of suspects yet. But I can't rule out that she is trying to help me solve this."

"Okay, but first you need a good night's sleep and we have a show to put on for the bishop tomorrow. At least the film crew wasn't following you today. Enchanted priest falls off scooter would be viral within twenty-four hours."

Time Spent With Cats

Poor Hugo eyeballed me from the step in front of the vicarage's front door. He hissed as I fumbled with the key in the lock. The tip of his tail curled and flicked as he sauntered across the threshold and down the hall. This was one hacked off pussy cat, and I needed to fill his food bowl double-quick.

There was only an hour left before my usual bedtime, but I needed to clear my mind before heading to sleep. Whilst Hugo was vacuuming up his dinner, I slipped upstairs and threw on my pyjamas. I took a beat to check my bruises in the full-length mirror of my wardrobe. I was very lucky. A slight bump was growing on the left side of my skull, but it only hurt to touch, and there was no blood.

Back downstairs, I made myself a mug of hot chocolate and reclined on the sofa in the morning room. I aimed the remote control at the television and settled back to watch some mindless entertainment.

Hugo snuggled his head under my elbow and curled up on my lap. His internal motor purred.

"Am I forgiven now? I understand. You were *hangry*. I'm sorry."

The odour of tuna flakes in oil-rich jelly assaulted my nose. I wanted to throw up, but Hugo looked so comfortable. I had to hold my nerve and my stomach.

I switched on my phone and searched for ways to prevent vomiting. One website suggested sugary drinks. *Check.* And resting in a seated position. *Double-check.* I threw the phone to the side and concentrated on my hot chocolate and finding a programme to watch. *Preferably something without witches.*

I found an old series of the *Great British Bake Off.* No pagan rituals or mysterious dead bodies there.

Perfect.

Either the smell of Hugo's dinner had worn off, or my olfactory senses had grown more accustomed to the scent, but whichever, I was as chilled as a Japanese macaque relaxing in a hot spring bath by the end of the Technical Challenge. *Hmm, brandy snaps.*

"So, my fluffy friend, what do we know?"

Hugo struck out his front legs and clawed my thigh. Then folded them back under his body, ready for a long sleep.

"You're right. We should rest." I rubbed the back of his head.

"Shelta Lee has the most obvious motive. I am struggling to link anyone else to a stronger reason to want Kat Pringle dead. Shelta had time and opportunity. I would say she was fit enough to hold a pillow down over someone's face. And she has an artistic flair that could explain the tiara and fixing her hair."

I swallowed the final powdery mouthful of chocolate. Only the unmixed sediment remained at the bottom of my mug.

"But then why enchant me? If not to help me find Kat's killer, what was the point?"

A puff of air interrupted the GBBO showstopper judging and my musings.

Hugo's rear end had released a distinct odour. *Tuna and cabbage doughnuts?*

I screwed my mouth shut and held my nose.

Seriously, cat. You're asleep!

"Maybe Shelta just wanted to see me suffer? Her parlour trick hasn't exactly given me much luck so far."

Hugo purred on my lap, unaffected by his windy bottom, or my suppositions.

"Any right-thinking person would place Shelta Lee at the crime scene, murder weapon in hand, but so far it's all conjecture. My gut says it wasn't her, but all roads currently lead to Elton's village witch. I need proof. Hard evidence. Like Kat's headphones or mobile phone."

I stroked Hugo's ear. I loved the way it would flick back each time.

"And to think I was once allergic to cats. Coming home to Wesberrey has changed so many aspects of my life."

I bent over to kiss my feline friend's triangular head.

"So, Shelta is still a suspect. Yemi was also out that night. Where did he go? What did he do? Why would you take a scooter out along dark country roads when you don't know where you are? And was I too rash to count out Muriel? Maybe she's sprightlier than I think?"

Hugo curled his tail around his legs.

I closed my eyes.

*****

When I opened them again, the television was judging me, and the sun was rising.

I picked up the remote and scrolled down to 'No, I have finished watching' and hit enter. Hugo was mewing at the door to be let out. I stretched and rolled myself forward.

Assembly was at half nine and Tobias and friends were to meet me at the school. It was now seven o'clock, plenty of time for a shower and breakfast.

Since Mum had left, our adopted vegan lifestyle, designed to support the development of the Dungeons and Vegans menu, had gone awry. I found I was too chaotic a cook, or too lazy, to prepare nutritious vegetable dishes. However, I could throw some mushrooms, onions, and tomatoes in a pan with a couple of eggs and make for myself a cracking good *vegan* dish. Free range, of course. From a local farmer. Delivered fresh each morning on the milk round.

The milk round!

I had never taken much notice of when I receive my deliveries, but they must pass by the vicarage around five in the morning. Wish I had thought of that last night. I could have asked if the farmer remembered picking up Amy that morning. As Scarlett O'Hara said, 'Tomorrow is another day.'

A bouquet of fried onion caramel goodness, sweet tomatoes, and earthy mushrooms rose from the pan. A black hairball wearing a crown of bronze leaves followed the scent of omelette de la Jessamy in from the back garden. The sun's eager rays followed behind, lighting up the kitchen.

"This isn't for you, fluff bag. You're becoming a bit of a chunky boy." I pushed his full dish under his face with my foot. "That's yours. Gourmet kitty grub, only the best for you."

Hugo disagreed. Stuck his black nose in the air and turned his back on me.

"Suit yourself. Some people are impossible to please."

Being able to smell more intensely had one added benefit. My food tasted even better than usual. All the aromas danced around my mouth and images, or rather memories of other meals and events where I had eaten the same ingredients, popped into the forefront of my mind.

Fried tomatoes overlooking a white sandy beach with my father and grandparents. Must have been at their villa in Portugal. I don't remember having been there, but the memory was so vivid.

Mushroom omelettes at my flat in London after bartending all night after a full day at drama school. Laughing so much with my flatmate that I cracked the eggs onto the stove, missing the pan.

Zuzu burning the onions for the Sunday roast. She would have been about fourteen. She tried to persuade us that the charred black offerings were how the top chefs were cooking them now.

Every recollection tasted as real as the omelette on my plate. I could reach out and touch the people I was with. And I wanted to. I really did.

Old memories can attach to themselves powerful emotions, even those buried so deep within us we aren't consciously aware of ever making them. Yemi and Kat had a relationship in the past. It may have been, as Yemi said, a brief fling many years ago, but maybe it was extremely passionate, or painful. Who knows what buried hurts or secret longings their meeting again brought to the surface.

Kat performed a 'Come to me' spell. There was a high probability it was for Yemi. My natural scepticism would normally say this was bunkum. But during the past twelve or so hours, I had seen, or rather smelt, first-hand, the magical possibilities of this ancient craft.

If I can believe that I will be the next godmother of a triple goddess, then this is an easy stretch.

I could also imagine that dragging someone out of their cosy four-poster bed to ride out in the dark, destination unknown, wouldn't be the best start to rekindling an old relationship.

I needed to find a way to talk to Yemi alone.

Cauliflower's Fluffy

Bishop Marshall and Archdeacon Faulkner arrived at the vicarage just before nine.

"Archdeacon! What a pleasant surprise. I wasn't expecting you as well."

"I sent you an email. But I guess you have been busy with a film crew in tow."

"Well, I would offer you both some refreshments, but we need to get to the school. I'm sure we can sort out a cup of tea or something there. Then, perhaps a brunch at my sister's cafe? You must have had a very early start."

Bishop Marshall bowed. "Thank you for your offer, Jessamy, but we will need to be back on the mainland by noon. Another time, perhaps. Lead the way."

The three of us shuffled across the churchyard like a group of migrating penguins. I think the walk comes from wearing cassocks to work. One learns to take measured steps to appear graceful and authoritative in a long dress. Heaven help us if we caught a heel or a toe in the skirt's hem when processing across the altar.

"Your Grace, it's not too late to refuse permission to the TV crew. I am not happy with the direction they are taking the programme. I fear it will be pure sensationalism and very damaging for the church."

"But Faulkner here led me to believe that you are good friends with the star. What's his name again?"

"Tobias Dean. Yes, I knew him years ago. But he is looking for the next big hit show and thinks this could be it. Like one of those trashy reality TV shows. I am not happy for it to continue."

"Hmm, I will take your concerns under consideration. I understand your reluctance to be the face of the modern church, but if God has chosen you, my dear, who am I to stop it?"

That is not my biggest worry!

Tobias waited by the gate to greet our special guests.

"Your excellency, please step this way."

"Dear boy, please address me as My Lord. Save the excellency for the Archbishop."

"A thousand apologies, my lord." Tobias shot a wink in my direction. "I am sure the Archbishop will be delighted with our little programme. I do hope you will spare some time after the show to do a small piece for the camera. Talk about the lovely reverend here."

"We shall see. My priority is watching these wonderful cherubs celebrating God's bounty."

Tobias handed my clerical superiors over to Amy's eager care and hung back to catch a word or two with me. "Who knocked the sweets out of his pinata this morning? Is he always this much fun?"

"Mmm-hm," I replied. Tobias had gained a cut above his right eyebrow. "Speaking of pinatas, looks like someone mistook you for one. Who'd you fall out with this time?"

"No one. I fell out of the bed, hit the post. Not my finest hour." Tobias grinned.

"But you, Reverend Ward, have been holding out on me. He may be officious, but that voice! The audience will lap him up. That Faulkner guy is a trifle too serious, though. Not sure there's a need to interview him." Tobias clapped his hands together. "Right! Let's get this show on the road."

"Assembly, not show."

"Yeah, right, Got yah!"

I sneaked past the rows of cross-legged children to the front of the hall, where Lawrence was already holding court from the wooden block dais in front of the fold-away gym equipment.

Once everyone was in position, the choir sang 'All things bright and beautiful'. Some of the more confident members of Year Six presented a short PowerPoint presentation about starving children in Africa before the Reception class broke into a rousing rendition of 'Cauliflowers fluffy' as they held up placards with painted pictures of strawberries, cabbages, beetroots and so on. Then Lawrence spoke a few words about the ancient practice of gleaning.

"In days gone by, when the wheat was ready for harvest. Farmers would hire reapers. Skilled men with scythes—"

"Like the Grim Reaper, Sir?" a cheeky voice called out from somewhere in the centre.

"Yes, Kai, just like the Grim Reaper, except he harvests souls, and these guys were content with cereal. Anyway, the reapers would cut down and gather up as much wheat as they could in one pass of the field. Whatever they missed on that first pass, they left behind for the poor widows and orphans, or for foreign travellers, to take as they needed. They called this gleaning. Do you think this is something we should still do today?"

A bunch of eager hands shot up toward the ceiling. One child in the front row reached so high, she almost lost her balance.

She's just so cute!

Lawrence couldn't resist.

"Jade, what do you think?"

"I think we should leave it for the animals. The badgers and the hedgehogs and the raccoons."

"Jade, there are no racoons in England."

"Because they've all starved to death!" shouted a lone voice from the back.

Everyone laughed.

My turn next. *How am I going to follow that?*

"Mr Pixley is right. There are no raccoons in Great Britain. Never has been. But there was a time when our lands teemed with bears, wild hogs and even wolves. We hunted them all to extinction, and now we are stealing the habitat of many of God's beautiful creatures across the world. So many species are endangered. Elephants, tigers, pandas. We also have many widows and orphans fleeing war in their home countries, and we have families here who struggle to make ends meet."

I looked out at the sea of angelic faces. This island's, this county's, this country's, even the world's future sat in rows before me. A part of my soul grieved for the earth that is already lost to them.

"This Sunday, over in St. Bridget's Church, we will be formally receiving the gifts of food you and your families have kindly donated to help your neighbours who do not have enough to eat. We will sing songs as we have this morning, and say prayers, to tell our heavenly Father how grateful we are for what he has given us. I want you to close your eyes."

Two hundred little faces squeezed their eyes into raisins. Some tried to cheat by keeping one slightly open, but a stern look from the nearest teacher closed even the most rebellious lids.

"Now I want you to think about the person or thing you love most. Maybe it's your mother, or your dog, or your football. I don't care. Just think about how much you love them. How grateful you are to have them in your life. And thank God in your heart for giving them to you. For letting you enjoy time with them. When you are done, raise your hand."

One by one, hands crawled upwards.

"Okay, looks like you are all finished. On the count of three, I want you to all shout thank you at the top of your voices. I want you to scream thank you so hard that the cats on the harbour will hear you. Then we will all open our eyes. Ready? One...two...three."

THANK YOU!

Bishop Marshall applauded from the wings. As he glided towards the stage, I stepped aside.

"Well, well, my dears. I think they heard that all the way to Stourchester!" Beaming with joy, the bishop's pride scanned across every child, like a lighthouse illuminating the waters.

"I wanted to say thank you for a wonderful morning. Your beautiful singing. That impressive presentation. You are all so very clever." Many of the children giggled. The bishop's sonorous voice created much the same reaction with adults as well. A unique combination of depth and tone that resembled a very large Tibetan singing bowl.

Unperturbed, he continued. "I think the most important thing that Jesus, our Saviour, ever gave us was his commandment to love one another as I have loved you. Or, as I believe you trendy young things say these days, hashtag Be Kind."

Pupils and teachers sniggered.

"Just one thing before I go. Can we all sing that cauliflower song again?"

*****

I missed my chance to speak to Yemi as Tobias whisked him and Dev away to film the Bishop before he left. Archdeacon Faulkner, it seemed, was surplus to requirements. Amy found a use for him, though, signing waiver forms and feeding her details about the church's current view on spiritualism and the afterlife. The archdeacon would keep her busy for quite some time.

A familiar aftershave floated over from behind me, a gentle hand on my shoulder followed, then warm breath nuzzled at my ear.

"Are you feeling better this morning?"

The voice of my dreams. I turned to face Lawrence.

"Yes, I am perfectly fine. Can still smell your cologne. Did you shower or just bathe in Paco Rabanne?"

"Well, I usually wash in ass's milk, but the grocery store was all out."

I slapped his chest. "You're so droll. I thought the assembly went very well. The bishop seemed pleased."

"Yes, the children were on their best behaviour. But I did promise them all an extended lunch break if they were good." he smiled.

"Ah, you are so cunning."

"As cunning as a fox who's just been appointed Professor of Cunning at Oxford University?" Lawrence tilted his head and scrunched his mouth into a pout.

"Is that a quote from Blackadder?" I snorted. I pretended to stamp my feet. "Does that make me Baldrick?"

"Yes, Blackadder Goes Forth, and I believe it does. But I loved his fuzzy little sidekick." Lawrence flipped a loose strand of hair behind my ear.

"Tony Robinson is a national treasure. But I saw you more as the Hugh Laurie character, rather than Blackadder himself."

"He became something of a sex symbol when he starred in House, so I'll take that." He stroked his hand along my cheekbone.

A forced cough to our left crushed our special moment.

"You lovebirds are just so cute. We need to film the two of you together. We could fit you in tomorrow morning. Jess, do you still do your weekly exercise group?"

"Er, yes, with Wesberrey Walkers, but I missed the classes this week. What with the seance and then last night."

"Oh?" Amy bit the top of her pen. "What happened last night?"

I glanced at Lawrence. My face pleaded *cover for me*. "I cuddled up with the big guy here."

"Really? And you weren't in Oysterhaven General then?"

How did she know that?

"Er..."

"I bumped into the dishy Inspector during my run. He was collecting your scooter from the ferry. Seems the police took care of it for you overnight." Amy sneered. "He said you had an accident, and he was going to call on you this afternoon."

"Did he? Really? Well... yes, that was earlier. Just a few bruises. I spent the rest of the evening with Lawrence."

"Yes, I brought her home." Lawrence looped his arm around my waist and squeezed tight.

"Oh, okay. As long as you're not hurt." Amy's phone rang. "Sorry, I need to get this." She answered and asked the person on the other end to hold on. "Just one question. What were you doing in Oysterhaven? You didn't have an appointment in your diary?"

I cannot tell a lie.

"Visiting Shelta Lee at her shop in Elton."

Lawrence's tightening grip almost ruptured my spleen.

"Ooh, is she your prime suspect? Great stuff. I have to get this, but we'll chat later. Okay?" Amy leaned in and planted an air kiss about an inch away from my face.

"Did you get that?" I turned to Lawrence and sniffed his cologne. "It's gone now."

"What has?"

"I'm not sure, but I think it's time to do some super sleuthing."

A Matter for the Police

T obias released the bishop into my charge about twenty minutes later. He wanted to get some shots of the island, particularly at sunset, as the 'right' weather was predicted. According to Yemi, the recent sunny spell was to give way tomorrow to rain, and such change in frontal systems leads to cirrus clouds that create the most dramatic sunset images.

I learnt something new.

Also, the predicted rain would make for gloomy background shots tomorrow, so the crew was keen to spend the entire afternoon getting as much footage as they could.

"You know what that means?" I whispered to Lawrence.

Lawrence furrowed his brow. "Er, no. Not following."

"It means they won't be in their rooms at the Cat and Fiddle."

"Jess, that's a terrible idea."

"I have nothing else to go on." I checked over my shoulder. "If it's not Shelta, it has to be Yemi. He might still have her phone in his room."

"Jess—"

"Ah, Reverend Ward. I'm ready to go now. So sorry I can't stay for lunch. But duty calls. Mr Pixley thank you. The children were adorable. Come on now Faulkner, chop, chop."

Saved by the bishop!

*****

The horse-drawn taxi dropped Bishop Marshall and Archdeacon Faulkner at the ferry port, and I skipped to the pub, a hundred yards away. I found Phil in the kitchen overseeing the lunchtime service.

"Vicar, what are you doing here? Am I on camera?"

"No, Phil. I shook them loose. I was wondering if you could do me a favour?"

I explained to Phil that I needed to get access to Yemi's bedroom. Ideally, he would let me into all four rooms, but I had no grounds to search anyone else's.

"That sounds like a police matter, Vicar."

"Yes, it is. But they need a warrant and that takes days to get, and Kat Pringle's killer could be hundreds of miles away by then. All evidence destroyed."

"You really think it could be the big guy? He seems like such a gentle soul. Now that Tobias fella. I'd bet good money on him bein' involved."

"Why's that?"

"Well, he's very ambitious. What would make for a better show? Following a crime-fighting vicar when there's no crime or one when there is?"

My verger made an excellent point.

"So, Phil. Will you help me?"

He agreed, and moments later, I held the master key and the power to enter all the rooms. I needed to be quick, as the maid was due on shift in half an hour. Phil agreed to text me if any of the suspects came back early.

Yemi's first. His wardrobe was full of t-shirts and jeans. All the same size and make - just different colours. Like a uniform for life. I searched through his trouser pockets; the jacket flung over the back of the dressing table chair; and in all the drawers and found nothing.

Of course, he could have disposed of Kat's phone already or was carrying it in his camera bag. It's not really something you would leave lying around for the police, a maid, or an inquisitive priest to find.

The same again in Dev's room next door. No trace of a phone or headphones, but if I ever need to source tops with iconic bands from the eighties and nineties, then he's my man. The only other thing of interest was a slimline briefcase on the floor by his bedside cabinet. I lifted it up onto the bed and tried to flip open the locks. I tried the obvious combination codes, 0000 and 1234 with the expected outcome. Dev was too tech-savvy not to have unique passwords.

Next, I popped into Tobias's room. I looked out the window onto the square below. This spot was where Avril would have stood that night when she saw Shelta entering the bakery. Avril was a few inches taller than me and might have had a better view, but I couldn't see the bakery.

I could see the Guildhall and beyond that Bits and Bobs, but I could only make out Rosie's cafe because of the bright paintwork through the pillars below the hall. The upper main body of the building under the clock tower obscured the rest of the shops on that side.

I suppose she could have seen Shelta pushing her bike past Bits and Bobs and just assumed she was heading to the Needhams. Anyway, I had a second witness that placed Shelta there at that time, and she admitted it to me herself.

I searched every nook and cranny. Tobias was the untidiest, so far. The sign of a creative genius, perhaps. Clothes, including used underwear, lay strewn over every surface. I dodged the most offensive items and found empty drawers behind them.

I pity the poor maid who has to clean this up.

I pulled up the mattress and ran my hand underneath. There was a faint scent from his bed sheets. I steeled myself to take a closer look, or rather sniff.

Musty body odour. Sweat. Ugh! Some other bodily fluid that will remain nameless. And something sweet. No, salty. That could be the sweat. This temporary gift is just as useless as any of my other ones.

I rested on the floor. My backside touching the bedside cabinet. My legs were in a wide V-shape in front of me.

This is pointless. There is no reason at all to suspect Tobias or any other member of the crew. The only person with a motive is Yemi, and that search drew a complete blank.

I rolled onto all fours to push myself up off the carpet. A white wire next to the wastepaper bin caught my eye. I crawled over. Earphones, not headphones, but these could be Kat Pringle's.

I tipped the contents of the bin on the floor between my outstretched legs. Chocolate bar wrappers. Three Kit Kats. *Tobias, you have a problem.* Scrunched up Post-It notes. A flyer for the seance. A ferry timetable. No phone.

Outside, I could hear the maid knocking on another door. I threw all the rubbish back in the bin. Bunged the earphones back where I found them and cracked open the bedroom door. Everything looked clear, so I made a dash for the back stairs.

I handed the key back to Phil.

"Did you find anythin', Vicar?"

"Nope. I couldn't get into Miss Turner's room. Can I come back later when the cleaning is done?"

Phil nodded. "Anything in Mr Dean's room?"

I hesitated. "Do you know where Inspector Lovington is right now?"

*****

A speed dial later and I was heading back out to Travellers Bay. I found Dave taking one last tour of the garden to check for any more clues. He had parked Cilla on the road outside.

"Thanks for the loan of your scooter."

"I don't believe I actually gave you permission to ride her. Isn't it time you got your own transport on the island?"

Dave dusted some earth from his brogues. "I'm working on it. Besides, I enjoy taking a carriage. Connects me with the locals. For example, did you know that Amy Turner takes the milk round out here every morning and jogs back?"

"Will you be miffed if I said yes?" I switched my puppy dog face into overdrive.

Dave leaned against a fence post. "Not if that's the only thing you have kept from me. Why don't we go inside, and you can catch me up. Okay?"

Over Kat Pringle's kitchen table, still cluttered with lavender and corn dollies, ribbons and twine, I told the inspector all about my visit to The Howlet's Wing, my heightened olfactory sense, and how Muriel was staying in my aunt's shepherd's hut that night.

"But I discounted her because I don't see how she could have trekked across the field in the dark, and she seemed genuinely upset."

"Okay. And this is the part where I remind you it's not your job to discount anyone. You should have told me about Muriel. I will go to see her tomorrow. Anything else?

"Did you know that Yemi, the cameraman, was in a relationship with Kat Pringle years ago?"

Dave leant back in his chair and folded his arms. His eye twitched.

"Well, he was."

My guilty eyes flitted around the room. No candles or incense burning here. The few tea lights she had were all battery operated and still flickering.

"He went out for a ride late that night, but I haven't had a chance to speak to him yet."

"Me neither, which isn't surprising as he wasn't on my list of suspects – until right now." He huffed.

"I'm sorry. I checked his room earlier. No sign of anything connecting him with Kat. There were earphones in Tobias's room, but —"

Dave raised his right hand. "Hold on, did you break into their bedrooms and rifle through their belongings? I should arrest you for trespassing, or breaking and entering."

"I didn't break in. Phil gave me his skeleton key."

"So, you have made him an accessory. Jess, this has got to stop!"

"You brought me in on this!"

"Yes, to do your sixth sense thing, not my job." The dining chair screeched across the wooden floor. Dave paced around the room, cursing under his breath.

"And the others?"

"Dev's was clean too, and I didn't have time to look in Amy's as the maid came."

"Did you touch the earphones?"

This is embarrassing.

"Maybe?"

"Jess!"

"I said I'm sorry. Look, I have this smell thing. It won't last forever. Maybe I can pick up on something that would help? Or sense something in the bedroom?"

Dave pulled a ball of blue plastic from his suit trouser pocket. "Gloves."

Love Potion No 9

"S o?"

"It's hard to smell anything other than lavender. The stuff is everywhere. You would think she'd have no trouble sleeping with this natural sedative all around her."

"I suppose it desensitised her, working with it all day. How could anyone make a living selling these things?" Dave picked up a mini lavender wreath.

"Perhaps that's why she stole Shelta Lee's ideas for her website."

"Yeah, Miss Lee mentioned that when I interviewed her. She also admitted to being here that night."

I stopped skimming my hand across Kat's shelves. "Why haven't you arrested her then?"

"Because she says she left Miss Pringle alive and well around one a.m. And several witnesses saw her back in town by two."

"Ah, you've spoken to Stanley Matthews."

"Yes. Now he's an upright citizen who informs the police if he has any information, unlike some people I could mention."

"Again, I said I'm sorry. Still, Shelta has a motive, opportunity and she fought with Kat earlier that day. She must be a prime suspect."

"Nope." Dave stood in the doorway, his moustache pursed. "Looks like I finally know something you don't."

I waited.

And waited.

"Well?"

Dave inspected an imaginary watch on his wrist.

"Well, what?"

I threw my blue latex-covered hands into the air in frustration. "Do you want me to beg? Is that it?"

He smirked.

"Fine, I'm going to sniff the bedsheets."

I knelt on the floor. My stomach immediately sought evasive action.

Ugh! Cadaver juices!

"The coroner determined she died early in the morning. Somewhere between four and six."

*****

I took a deep breath and squeezed myself down on the rug beside Kat's bed and lifted the bedsheets. Pulled out my phone and switched on the torch.

"Now where would one put a love spell?"

The light caught on some dust bunnies, a stray sock, and a few crumbs.

"The forensics team searched this whole place with a fine-tooth comb."

I leant on the edge of the bed for support. "Yes, but they were looking for something the murderer left behind, not something the victim had hidden."

I creaked my body back up to an upright pose, well as close to upright as I could comfortably manage. *I was only down there a few minutes!*

"Help me pull this out." I tugged at the bedframe. Dave grabbed the other side.

In the skirting board behind the bed was an oblong air vent, screwed into the wall.

"Worry not, I was a boy scout." Dave produced a Swiss Army knife from his inside jacket pocket. "Be prepared."

"Dib, dib, dib. I'm impressed."

He unscrewed the plate and reached inside the cavity.

"Is this what you are looking for?"

At the end of his arm was a two-inch clear glass bottle with a cork stopper. The top was sealed with pink wax.

"I guess the colour signals romantic love."

"Shall we look inside?" Dave carried the bottle out into the kitchen. "We can empty it onto a clean plate, then I can bag it up."

"Shouldn't you dust for prints first?" I asked.

"You really think anyone else would put this there? Here, I'll put it on the counter and take some photos first."

Dave took shots of the bottle from several angles and then broke open the seal with his penknife. The wax, the cork, and the contents fell onto the plate below. He used the tip of his knife to separate the items. Taking more photographs at every stage.

Sitting under a heap of powder and dried herbs rolled up into a half-inch scroll was a strip of lined paper. Dave took a pen from his breast pocket and used it to hold down one end as he curled out the rest with the blade. Two words were written in pen across the paper.

"Yemi Adongo."

"I think I need to have a chat with Mr Adongo."

*****

Evidence separated and bagged, we locked up Kat's house.

"So, your team never located her phone or a laptop?"

"No, she must have had a way to update her website." Dave climbed onto Cilla.

"Excuse me, you're riding pillion."

"It's illegal without a helmet, and we only have one." He smiled.

"Then you can walk." I pulled my helmet out of the caddy box in the rear.

Dave looked at the plastic bags in his hand and then at the long, dusty road ahead.

"Okay, just drive carefully."

We arrived back at Market Square around ten minutes later. I deposited my passenger on the corner.

"Thank you. And Jess, no more snooping around." Dave held up the evidence bags. "Okay, this is a significant find, but please let me handle it from here."

"Of course."

I waved farewell and headed straight for the delivery yard at the rear of the Cat and Fiddle.

*****

The kitchen was a chaotic mass of activity. I had never really spent much time behind the scenes at my favourite pub. Well, it's the only one on the island, but it would still be my favourite as two of my best colleagues and friends ran it.

As I waited for one of them to appear so I could get the master key to Amy's room, I offered a quick prayer of gratitude for their friendship.

Some friend you are, Jessamy Ward. You are asking them to help you break the law.

The cartoonish angel and devil in my head began a full-on debate. Whilst they argued, I recalled that earlier I had watched Phil take the key from a small cabinet behind the bar.

If I can take the key myself, no one else is guilty, right?

The biggest problem I could foresee was the danger of Amy walking in on me as I searched. I whipped out my phone and dialled her number.

Mini devil Jess had a cunning plan.

"Hi, Amy? Can you hear me? Where are you now? ... Oh, on the other side of the island. Great. Look, I have a busy weekend ahead with the harvest festival and everything, so I was wondering if you and the team would like to come over for dinner tonight. Lawrence will be there, and maybe you could film us together then?... Wonderful, don't expect anything too fancy. I know the guys want to catch the sunset, so I'll see you around eight?... Perfect. Bye."

Text Lawrence. Dinner. Mine. 7pm.

Now to get the key.

*****

Taking the key from the cabinet was a piece of cake. And if I were quick, I would have time for a cup of tea and something light at D & V before I headed back home.

As the maid had been, there were few clues to Amy's personality from the state of her room, though I didn't imagine it looked very different. Unlike the others, she appeared to live out of her suitcase. There was a meshed side that held her dirty items and she had neatly rolled the rest in the main compartment. Nothing decanted into drawers or hung up, except for the toiletries in the bathroom. The effect was impersonal, efficient, transitory.

I carefully took out the rolls from her case and felt them for phones or earphones. Nothing. The cupboards, pillows, sheets and mattress all yielded a big fat zero. I checked the towels in the bathroom, even though I knew the maid would have changed them earlier.

There was that scent again. Just a hint of herbs? *I'm getting Shelta's shop.* If a smell were a colour, this would be sage green. I took a deep breath in through my nostrils. Slightly musky. And... there's a note of something else. Fresh. Crisp.

I was sure it was the same scent as earlier. Certainly not Lawrence's Paco Rabanne. This was a feminine fragrance.

Amy must have been wearing perfume this morning.

I rooted through her medicine cabinet. *Wow, she's a huge fan of Jo Malone.* Three different fragrances stood proud on the top shelf. I tried them all one by one, but none matched what I had smelt earlier.

She must have it with her.

Mini-devil Jess was onto something. I just needed a way to separate Amy from her Prada bag.

Dinner at Eight

I whirled in and out of Dungeons and Vegans like a dervish, picked up some sweet treats for dessert and headed back to the vicarage as quickly as Cilla could take me. I needed to prepare a meal for six, and I can barely cope with a microwave dinner for one.

Fortunately, Mum had stocked my freezer with homemade goodies before she moved. All I had to do was find six matching dishes and work out how to use the oven. *Vegetarian cottage pie it is!* Frozen green beans and some salad for garnish. It was a feast fit for royalty.

I laid out the mahogany table in the dining room. Used all the best crockery and silverware. Even found some unopened bottles of red wine at the back of a cupboard.

Lawrence was the first to arrive. *Well, I told him an hour earlier.*

"We have guests. I strongly suspect one of them is the killer. Probably Yemi, maybe Amy, but I'm not sure what her motive would be. And, I don't want to say it, but Tobias is also in the frame."

"But not the sound guy?" Lawrence teased.

"No, nothing points to Dev being involved. But Dave has ruled out Shelta Lee. Seems Kat Pringle died between four and six in the morning. And there are at least two witnesses that put her in the square at two a.m. I found earphones in Tobias's room. And Amy's perfume. I'm sure that's a clue."

VESTRY VICE

"Hold on. Back up a bit. What were you doing in your ex's bedroom?"

"Looking for incriminating evidence, silly. Are you jealous?"

I enjoyed the look on his face as he responded. "Not in the slightest." Lawrence pressed his lips against my forehead. "So, Reverend Ward, what scheme are you plotting for this evening?"

*****

"Sorry, we're late." Tobias crossed my threshold with an arm full of alcoholic beverages. "But your friendly neighbourhood copper was interrogating my bestie Yemi. We couldn't just leave him there. No man left behind that's my motto."

Lawrence relieved my ex of some of his bottles. "I believe that saying belongs to the U.S. military."

"I'm in good company then." Tobias leant back out the door to call to the others. "Get a move on."

"Not to worry. Nothing spoiled. Well, no more than it was half an hour ago. Let me take your coats. I will put them all upstairs."

Tobias shook his jacket off his shoulders, and I pulled it back.

"Hmm, you're going to throw them in a pile? Nothing says party more than that, eh? The things we used to get up to on a mountain of coats back in the day... ssh, mum's the word, eh? Not in front of the boyfriend."

I hooked the jacket over the banister. "Tobias, have you been drinking?"

"Just something to ward off the cold. The ride here has a terrible effect on my chest."

The rest of the party traipsed in one by one. And one by one, I took their coats and bags.

"I'm so pleased you could make it. Lawrence will get you seated in the dining room, and I'll take these safely upstairs. Dinner will be ready in a few minutes."

135

As they filed into the room, I gathered up their stuff. There was absolutely no need to move any of it from the hall, other than the activity gave me more time to go through their things upstairs whilst my beau kept our guests entertained.

There was nothing in anyone's pockets, which left the two bags. One was Dev's, and the other one Amy's.

I had to find the perfume, so I opened Amy's padded pink number first.

There it was. Jo Malone, London, Wood Sage and Sea Salt.

Lavender and sea salt!

I took off the silver cap and sprayed a mist close to my face. I inhaled deeply. Wood Sage and Sea Salt was definitely the scent from earlier. The same one I had noticed in Tobias's room. The same as the one in her bathroom.

This doesn't prove she is the murderer. Think, Jess, think.

Did Amy have time to catch the milk round out to Travellers Bay, break into Kat's house, suffocate her, and jog back before breakfast? Maybe. But why? I had no motive.

So, what if she wears perfume with the fragrance of sea salt? No jury in the land would prosecute anyone on something that could be a mere coincidence. And certainly not based on a hunch, fuelled by a witch's spell and propagated from a conversation with a dead person!

I didn't have the phone, or a laptop, or anything to place Amy in Kat's house that morning and absolutely no motive.

I replaced the bottle where I found it and opened Dev's brown canvas duffle bag. Except it wasn't a duffle bag. It was a rollout utility holdall, with multiple compartments for various tools and gadgets.

This is cool. Why had I not seen this before?

Most of the spaces were empty, so looking through took very little time. In a canvas flap, held secure by a woven strap, was a mobile phone. I pulled it out with the tips of my nails. The case had a picture of a glittery white unicorn.

I think I've just found Kat Pringle's phone.

*****

I pushed the phone back into its slot and sat on the edge of the bed in shock. Nothing had prepared me to consider Dev as a suspect. *I suppose it could be his own phone?* People are complex characters, however, I doubt a fan of eighties grunge would walk around with a horned version of My Little Pony on his phone case.

Maybe he was looking after the phone for someone else? Maybe he borrowed his sister's or girlfriend's or... I knew I had to tell Dave what I had found. First, I needed more to go on. The police can't search without a warrant. I had to give them probable cause.

I went downstairs and plated up the food. A homemade meal, good company, and free-flowing wine might help loosen a few tongues.

"Do you need any help?"

I almost jumped into the sink.

"Oh, Amy. Thank you, but I'm nearly there. I don't do a lot of entertaining, so everything's taken twice as long as I thought. Just mixing the salad."

Amy joined me at the chopping board. Her perfume curled around me, teasingly, like it knew what I was thinking.

"Yeah, not really something you can do in advance unless you want soggy lettuce." She giggled.

"And no one wants soggy lettuce." A grimace was as close to a smile as I could muster.

"So kind of you to invite us, especially when you are so busy. Running around the island. Doing God's work. Investigating murders." Amy took handfuls of shredded iceberg leaves and sprinkled them over the waiting side bowls.

"Reverend Jess, I hope you don't think me rude, but I thought you would have been all up into sleuthing what happened to the corn dolly maker and yet, here we are instead filming cute kids singing Ave Maria."

"All things bright and beautiful." I corrected her. "What did you think I would do? Don a trilby and search for clues with a giant magnifying glass?"

"Well, that would work better on camera." She picked up two bowls. "Shall we go through?"

I put three plates on a tray and followed close behind.

A few kitchen runs later, we were all sitting around the table, chomping through Mum's mashed potato and soya mince creation. Everyone seemed to enjoy it, though the frozen beans were a tad overcooked.

"So, Yemi. What did the inspector want to talk to you about?"

Tobias reached a hand across the table towards his friend. "You don't need to answer that, Buddy."

Yemi refilled his glass and took a sip. "No, I want to. Unlike some, I ain't got nothing to hide."

He balanced his knife and fork on his plate and placed both forearms, palms down, on the table.

"Seems Kat put a spell on me." Yemi studied the group's reactions. "Can you believe that? A love spell with my name on it and she hid it behind her bed."

"Did it work?" Lawrence asked, stuffing half a tomato in his mouth.

Yemi raised his glass to his lips. "I guess so."

"Is that where you went that night? Did you answer her siren call?"

I probably gave too much insight away, but I was desperate to know.

"I mean, Phil mentioned you took the scooter out late and didn't see you come back."

Amy sat back in her seat, arms folded. "So, you have been sleuthing, after all. I knew it."

"It came up in conversation." I swatted away her words with my hand.

"You don't say." Tobias put down his glass with a soft thud. "I think you've been holding out on us, Jess. Sneaking off and doing your own investigation when the cameras aren't rolling. And there was me, all naïve, thinking you were busy attending to your flock. Reciting made-up incantations to your breed of god to make people feel better."

"I was having a casual conversation with my verger, that's all."

"This same verger who just happens to be our landlord? What else did he tell you, eh?"

I took a gulp of wine. *Don't mention Avril and Verity.* "Nothing, I promise."

Amy leaned forward, the glint of the hunt in her eyes. "But you visited Shelta Lee. You got the jump on us there. We're only visiting her shop tomorrow. And you want us to believe your little jaunt was merely a pastoral visit?"

"Yes, it was."

"Right," said Tobias. "We need to recreate those scenes. Shame the lighting will be so different. Yemi, can you do some magic to make it all blend?"

The cameraman shrugged. I had hijacked his story.

"Yemi, I'm sorry. You were telling us about the love spell. Please go on."

He sighed. "I think the moment's gone, don't you?"

Dev raised his glass and pointed it towards his friend. "Here's to you, bro. I, for one, want to hear what happened next. Cause no girl has ever wanted me that bad. And we still have dessert to get through."

"Okay, if you insist." Yemi resumed his storytelling pose. Forearms on the table, palms down. "Like I said, I guess it worked because something made me restless. I couldn't sleep, so I went for a ride. Man, the roads are dark 'round here. It was kinda spooky."

"Where did you go?" I asked.

"Oh, just around. The Wesberrey Road loops right? I crashed in some fisherman's hut about a mile or two down the road. Hearing the waves lapping against the shore was so restful. The next thing I knew, I was being woken up by some crusty old sea dog who wanted his lobster pots."

Dev laughed. "So, my friend, the spell didn't work!"

"Not so sure about that. I dreamt about her. Kat. I wanted to go find her when I woke up. I just didn't know where she lived. I figured Amy would have her address on the waiver form, so it could wait. So, I went back for a shower before breakfast. I stank of fish. And, well, you know what happened next."

Lawrence peeped at me over his wineglass. "Time for dessert, I think."

"Yes, of course. Just one thing, Yemi. Did you tell Inspector Lovington all of this?"

"Of course, the fisher guy can give me a rock-solid alibi."

The Mummy

I got up to fetch the desserts, and Dev offered to help me.

Once in the kitchen, I opened the fridge to retrieve Rosie's vegan fruit tarts. Over the gentle whirring of the fridge, I clearly heard a metallic click behind me. The hairs on the back of my neck stood to attention.

I left the tarts and stepped back. There was a carving knife on the counter just out of arm's reach.

Jess, this needs to be smooth. Like a ninja.

I jumped, snatched the handle, and pivoted back around to face my assailant.

"Whoa, whoa, whoa! Hey, Reverend, I just wanted to chat."

Dev gestured to the closed door behind us.

"I'm sorry, I heard a click and—"

"You thought I had a gun?"

"Or a flick knife." My nervous laugh turned into more of a snort.

Realising I needed to turn my back to get out the desserts, I asked Dev if he could get them. He obliged.

"The icing sugar is in the cupboard over there." I pointed with the knife over his right shoulder.

Sugar collected, Dev unscrewed the canister and waved it over the tarts. "I guess you want me to sprinkle this over the plates?"

"If you would be so kind. Thank you." I steadied myself on the edge of the table. "Do you think everyone wants coffee?"

"Probably." He smiled. "Rev, I wanted to talk to you about Kat Pringle."

I reverse manoeuvred to the electric kettle and flipped the switch. The carving knife still waving in Dev's general direction. "What about her?"

There was a rapid knock at the door.

"Everything alright in there? Need any help?"

It was Lawrence, my knight in an argyle sweater.

"Come in, we were just waiting for the kettle." I hid the knife behind my back. "Look, why don't you two boys take the desserts through, and I'll bring in the coffee when it's ready."

I ushered them out into the hallway and watched them go into the dining room. A tear, or twenty, of pure relief, streamed down my cheeks. Dev knew something. Maybe he'd found that mobile phone. Perhaps I wasn't the only person playing detective.

Cafetière of boiling water and ground java bean ready, I added a jug of almond milk to the tray and took a deep, fortifying breath before re-entering the lion's den.

Tobias was regaling the dinner party with tales of his time in San Quentin.

"The crew followed me during the day, but at night it was just me and my GoPro. Being locked in a maximum-security prison with over two thousand murderers and violent gang members was not my idea of a spa date. You know what I mean?"

"Yes, but you got an Emmy nomination for that series," Amy fawned.

"And I won the BAFTA. I was at the table next to Dame Maggie Smith. She was very gracious about my award."

Amy skewered a strawberry on the end of her fork. "Your acceptance speech was so funny. When you thanked the guards for watching your back in the shower block."

Yemi huffed. "Yeah, it was hysterical." He placed his hands together as if he was about to pray. "Reverend, I have enjoyed my meal, but it's been a long day. Would it terribly offend you if I headed back now?"

"Of course not. I totally understand."

"I think that's our cue to head back to the ranch. Been a great evening, Jess." Tobias wiped a serviette across his mouth. "Lawrence, she's a keeper. You know that, right?"

"Oh, I know." Lawrence pushed back his chair. "Let me get your coats."

Moments later, we gathered in the hallway. I helped Dev with his bag. "I love this, it's most unusual."

"Oh, it's modelled on Brendan Fraser's utility bag in The Mummy. It's so practical. It has lots of handy pockets. Keeps me organised."

I patted Dev on the shoulder. "One of my favourite films. I loved the bit when Evie knocks down all the bookshelves. It's exactly the sort of stupid thing I would do."

"But she was incredibly clever." Dev fixed me in his gaze. "She worked it all out in the end."

"And she was stunningly beautiful." Tobias rallied his troops. "Right chaps, let's go. Jess, let's reschedule you and the golden boy here for tomorrow evening. Does that suit?"

Tobias didn't wait for a reply. "We have a date with a full-on witch tomorrow. Need to watch yourself, Yemi. Don't want you falling under any more love spells, now do we?"

*****

Lawrence, perceptive as always, caught that he had walked into a situation in the kitchen.

"I can sleep in the guest room," He offered.

"What would the neighbours say?" I tiptoed my lips to his handsome face and kissed him.

"Tom and Ernest? I think they would put out the flags!" He kissed me back.

"Exactly. We'd be the talk of the island by breakfast."

"Okay, but soon I'm going to make an honest woman out of you. I quite fancy being the vicar's wife. Coffee mornings, whist drives."

"Hmm, I think a gingham apron would suit you." One last kiss. "Okay, off you go."

"Are you sure?"

I hesitated. Mini devil Jess prodded me with her fork. *The spare bedroom, that's okay, right?*

Lawrence brushed away a stray hair caught on my mascara. "Jess, I'll go home, if that's what you want. I will whistle as I leave, so any nosy passer-by can give me an alibi."

My fingers walked up his chest. "Well, if you pulled your finger out and proposed, we wouldn't need to do this."

"All in good time, my love."

And with that, he walked out into the starry night. I remained in the doorway until he disappeared around the corner onto Upper Road. The memory of his kiss lingered on my lips. A soft, furry slinky wrapped around my ankles.

"Hey, Hugo. Where have you been hiding all night? It's time for bed."

Despite, or perhaps because of, the red wine with dinner, sleep was elusive. I reached for my phone. *Perhaps I should try listening to an Amazonian rainforest or crashing waves? It seems to work for everyone else.* I hit play on the app and snuggled back into my pillow.

Raindrops tap danced on leaves to a backtrack of rolling thunder. It was hypnotic. My heart slowed to the natural rhythm of the jungle. My breath, deep and calm. Through the forest, a lone drum beat louder and louder. Its tempo rushed and out of time.

Wake up Jess, there's someone at the door!

I fumbled with my phone in the dim light. Volume down, the banging continued. I grabbed my dressing gown from the end of the bed and went down to investigate. The sound was coming from the kitchen. Hugo ran ahead of me. I almost tripped over him in the dark.

A shadow stood at the other side of the back door. I switched on the light and took the knife from the worktop.

"Hugo, get back here!"

"Reverend Ward. Please, it's me. Dev. Let me in."

*****

I unbolted the locks and picked up my feline friend before opening the door. Knife still in hand, I held Hugo close to my chest with my other arm. Not sure what would be more intimidating: a thrusting knife or a flying cat.

"Not the knife again. Reverend, I'm not going to hurt you." Dev shuffled into the kitchen and pulled out a chair. As he sat down, I closed the back door and set Hugo down on the table. The poor thing clearly annoyed at being woken from his slumbers.

He isn't the only one.

I sat in the chair at the other end of the table.

"Okay, you have my undivided attention. You wanted to talk to me about Kat Pringle."

Sugar on Top

"**I** found something."

"Oh?"

Can't think what it could be.

"Really? What did you find?"

"A phone." Dev lowered his head. "I think Amy took it from the victim's house."

"Where did you find it?"

"Remember when we went on that fishing trip. Tobias and Yemi were casting their rods over the side of the boat. It's not my jam, you know. So, I went up to the cabin to check out their sonar equipment and stuff. I know, I am such a nerd."

He paused and looked at the sink.

"May I have a drink of water, please?"

"Of course." I filled a glass and slid it across the table.

"Thank you. Well, I don't think Amy saw me go up there, but I saw her on the other side of the boat. She was throwing stuff off the side. I thought it was weird, so I watched her leave and went down to look."

"Did you see what she was chucking overboard?"

"No, she had her back to me. I didn't expect to find anything. You know. The current should have taken it away. But the phone had caught on some netting."

"And you retrieved it."

What are the chances?

"Yes. I was going to take it to the police, but these are my family. I couldn't believe Amy would kill anyone. She probably found it too, maybe on her morning run, I thought. And I dunno, maybe she didn't realise what she had or thought that she could get some information on the victim from it. You know?"

Dev's lips trembled. He bit down on his bottom one, but they continued to shake. The skinny fingers of one hand rubbed across his forehead and then his mouth, finally providing a resting place for his chin. The fingers of his other hand drummed continuously.

I wanted to offer some comfort. He looked terrified.

"The thing is though, Reverend. If she found it, why didn't she turn it in to the police? Why was she trying to get rid of it?"

Good question.

"Have you looked at the phone?" I asked. "How can you be sure it's Kat Pringle's?"

"Mm-hm, I unlocked it. There were loads of messages between her and Shelta Lee. Some missed calls from Amy. And photos of her with her purple hair and her corn dollies. The case has a sparkly horse thing on it. No way is that Amy's."

"No," I needed a glass of water myself. "You need to go to the police. I can call Dave to come here. Do you have the phone with you?"

147

Dev reached into his back pocket and laid the phone screen up on the table.

"Anything else you want to tell me before I call?"

"Just that I'm sorry. Sometimes, you know, Tobias... he... we can all get carried away. I shouldn't have recorded you and the inspector. But don't worry, I couldn't pick up anything till you opened the window. The conversation was pretty dry, to be honest. I doubt we would ever use it." Dev pulled a USB stick out of his inside jacket pocket. "Here. You should listen for yourself."

"Well, that's a relief." I smiled. "Just wait here. I need to get the inspector's number."

I called from the landline. We had Dave and Susannah's home number stored in a rotary address book on the hall stand. I figured I could just keep that ringing until he answered. Mobiles cut off too soon.

It took several minutes before Dave lifted the receiver at the other end. Though groggy, he agreed to come over straight away. Without his own transport, the inspector would have to walk. I needed to keep Dev occupied until he arrived.

I shuffled back to the kitchen.

The back door was ajar, and Hugo was about to step outside.

Dev had vanished.

The phone and dongle, though, remained on the table.

*****

"Did you touch them?" Dave snapped on his blue gloves and fiddled with a plastic bag.

"No, not really. I used my nails to look at the phone when it was still in Dev's holdall."

"Well, I will need to take your prints to eliminate you."

"And Dev's" I hovered vulture-like.

"Hmm, oh I will most definitely be taking Mr Patel's and a DNA swab too." Dave pulled off his gloves. "Bin?"

I pointed to the cupboard under the sink. "You don't think he was more involved, do you?"

"The phone caught in a net? All sounds fishy to me." He laughed at his own joke.

"Haha, so... are you going to see what's on the USB?"

"I'll leave that to the guys in the lab."

"Okay, it's just... aren't you curious to see if there is anything else on it?"

"Jess, as I said, I will give it to the guys at the lab."

"Or we could try it on my computer."

Despite my hunger for sleep, my need to find out what was on that file was more insatiable. I know I looked like an ogress dragged through a thicket, but now was the moment to deploy my well-honed feminine charms.

"Pleeeeease!"

Dave remained firm.

"Pretty please."

"Jess. No."

"Pretty please with sugar on top, that is my final offer."

Those puppy dog eyes that used to make my knees go weak, now narrowed under knitted brows.

"What time is it?"

"Coming up to four. The milk round will be here in just over an hour. You can cadge a lift back into town."

He huffed. "How strong can you make your coffee?"

"Hmm, somewhere between nuclear and volcanic."

Dave considered his options. From his coat pocket, he produced a fresh pair of gloves.

"You win. Do you have any syrups?"

*****

Like me, my ancient desktop struggled to function most mornings. I understood its reluctance to face a new day. Its memory overloaded with duties to perform and memories to process. There is so much to filter, we take longer and longer to fire up again. A disturbed night of downloading background applications and data management has not replenished us but drained us of valuable battery life. We are slower, but we can still do the job.

After logging in, Dave inserted the stick into the drive, and we waited for the computer to read the contents.

"It can be a little sluggish in the morning," I explained.

"I know how it feels." He cleared his throat. "Jess, I think it's time Zuzu met my family. The kids are keen to see what all the fuss is about. Do you think that will scare her off? Meeting my mother and my children. That's heavy stuff, right?"

"Dave, your mother is a baroness and lives on a country estate. Zuzu will think she is Lady Mary and act accordingly. As for your children, I know she can't wait to meet them."

A white square flashed on the screen. Dave peered over my shoulder.

"There are three sound files. Play the first one."

I right-clicked and adjusted the volume control. A faint muffled recording of Dave and me talking in Kat Pringle's bedroom drifted out from the built-in speakers.

My heart fluttered with relief. "Nothing incriminating there."

Dave pointed to the second file. I dragged my mouse across and hit to open.

"I did this for you!"

I looked at Dave. "That's Amy's voice."

"I didn't ask you to. You've gone mad."

"Is that Tobias Dean?" Dave grabbed the mouse and turned the volume up further.

The recording continued.

"I don't understand why you are so angry."

There were sounds of a kerfuffle.

Amy's voice returned.

"I'm sorry. I didn't mean to hurt you. I would never hurt you."

"Well, you did. Just get out... Get out!"

Then sobs, some shuffling sounds. A door opened and closed.

"Dev has been bugging his colleagues!" I gasped.

It's always the quiet ones.

"Sounds like they fought. Maybe that explains the cut over Tobias's eye?"

Dave perched his behind on the edge of my desk. "Looks that way. There's one more file. Open it."

This time the first voice was Yemi's.

"Why shouldn't I go straight to the police, eh? Is this how we get good ratings now, eh? Murder! Just one question, why Kat? Why choose someone I once loved?"

An awkward silence followed. The stillness was menacing. Whomever he was speaking to was keeping the motive to themselves.

It was Yemi who broke the silence.

"I get it. You're jealous. You want what I have with him. But that ain't never going to happen, and do you know why? Because he is my brother. My comrade. You will never be more than a means to an end." Yemi chuckled. "Everyone slips up somewhere, and when the police haul your sorry ass in, I will be there with a ring-side seat. Camera rolling. Enjoying every beautiful moment."

The Milkman Cometh

"**P**lay that again."

Your wish is my command, oh moustached one.

I played both clips again.

"It's Amy. She's the killer, and they all know. They all know."

The screen and everything around me blurred and faded to grey. A lump formed in my mouth, blocking a scream. They all knew. They sat around my dining table and pretended there was still a mystery to be solved.

Dave paced out his thoughts behind me.

"But how did she do it?"

I pivoted my chair to face him. "That's easy. She took the milk cart out, broke in, smothered Kat, had the cheek to do her hair to make the body camera ready and jogged back in time for breakfast."

I reminded Dave about the lavender and sea salt and explained about finding the Jo Malone fragrance in Amy's bag.

"But none of that is admissible as evidence. I need something more than some cryptic, and might I suggest illegal, recordings."

"Like earphones?" I exclaimed. "Maybe they're still on the floor in Tobias's room."

Dave stopped. Went to say something and thought better of it.

"I was searching his room. I looked around Amy's too, but there was nothing, and now I know why. She had already taken everything on the boat with her."

The pinball game in Dave's mind was bouncing ideas around. "So, the fishing trip was a ruse to go out to sea and get rid of any evidence. Who suggested it?"

"I'm sure Amy just took advantage of the situation. It can't have been some elaborate plot."

Dave stared me down. "Jess, who suggested it?"

"Tobias."

"And the earphones were in his room."

I didn't need to respond. It wasn't a question. Tobias was an accessory after the fact.

My next thought was almost unthinkable. "And Yemi?"

"My guess is he suspects but has no evidence. The soundman might have played him the recording. Even if Amy confessed to him, he'd stay loyal to Tobias."

My sleep-deprived brain struggled to put all the pieces together. "But why did Dev come to me? Why not go straight to you?"

"Why was he recording everyone to begin with? Insurance. Self-preservation."

"I need to get dressed. The milk cart will be here soon."

Dave smirked. "There's no point in telling you to go back to bed and leave this to the professionals?"

"Nope. Can you feed Hugo for me?"

*****

Dawn was still a full hour away. There was rustling in the trees and hedgerows as we passed. Creatures of the night returning to their lairs. Birds warming up for the morning's choir practice. A warm tinge on the horizon heralded the sunrise to come.

Dave sat shotgun upfront with the old farmer, quizzing him about the young lady who hitches a ride every morning from outside the pub. They stowed me in cargo with the farmer's grisly old sheepdog and crates of fresh dairy products. The dog had little to say but helped keep me warm. The morning breeze failed to clear my nostrils of his shaggy odour, but I welcomed his attentions. Autumn had arrived wrapped in woolly scarves and heated hand warmers. *A pumpkin latte would be so good right now.*

The inspector leaned back as we rounded the corner into Harbour Parade.

"Jess, keep your head down. We're going to stop as usual by the Cat and Fiddle and let Ms Turner come to us. Okay?"

My frozen nose signalled my agreement in the air.

"Have you asked him what time he usually arrives at Travellers Bay? Would she have had time? I mean, she took time to style Kat's hair and everything."

"We'd need to do a test run, but I think it's doable, just. Let's just ask her a few questions and go from there."

The cart drew up outside the pub. I slid down low behind some crates. I could hear Dave climbing down and greeting his prey.

"Miss Turner. What a pleasant surprise. I was hoping to find you at some point today. I thought perhaps we could have a chat."

"Er, Inspector Lovington. The crew is heading to the mainland today, but I will be back later this afternoon if you want to schedule a time."

The dog started licking my earlobe. I pushed him away.

"Actually, Miss Turner, I don't have much time this afternoon. Perhaps we could take advantage of this opportunity. I'm sure Phil will find us a table to talk privately."

Fido, or whatever his name was, was becoming a tad too amorous. I tried to wriggle free.

"I would love to, Inspector. But I was just about to go on a run. Can't keep this kind man waiting."

"Maybe over breakfast then? I love Phil's full English."

My slobbering canine admirer was pushing his luck. It was time to reject his advances with a tad more force. Extending my arms to hold him off I stared the creature down. *No means no, Fido!* Rejected, the dog whimpered and slunk behind another crate. *Aw! I'm such a bad person...* I felt awful but this was not the time or place.

"I'm sorry, Inspector, it will have to be this afternoon. I don't do breakfast."

She doesn't do breakfast! Barbara! That's the last time I listen to you.

Over my rattling thoughts, I could make out the sound of someone climbing into the seat next to the farmer.

Memories of how frightened and alone Kat was in her last moments flooded my mind.

I leapt up and clambered over the crates, screaming like a banshee.

"You killed Kat Pringle!"

Amy didn't react. She continued to stare ahead, motionless.

"You murdered an innocent woman to get better ratings?"

Still looking forward, with no discernible emotion, she replied.

"Netflix will love it."

Tell Me on a Sunday

There would be no more filming.

Dave took Amy away in handcuffs, as Yemi filmed from the pavement outside the pub. Afterwards, the rest of the crew were helping the police with their enquiries.

Be careful what you wish for, they say. I wanted to stop the programme. I had prayed on it every day, but now, as I prepared for Sunday service, I would do anything to change what happened.

The bell ringers, provided with brand new wrist supports, called to the faithful. The welcome dirge of Rosemary practising on the organ seeped down the corridor to the sacristy. A gentle knock on the door completed the symphony.

"Come in."

Ernest poked his head around the door.

"Ah, Reverend. Do you have a moment?"

"I always have time for you, my friend. How may I help?"

"Please, can we sit down?"

"Of course. Ernest, what's wrong?

"Reverend, I am sorry, but I have no choice other than to resign as churchwarden."

My heightened sense of smell may have waned, but all my other faculties were picking up a deep sadness in his words. I tried to make eye contact, but Ernest uncharacteristically averted my gaze.

"Ernest, please tell me what is happening."

At the PCC meeting, Tom was so upset. I feared the worst.

"I begin chemo next week. I need to put all my affairs in order first. There's so much to do. And Tom. You will keep an eye on him for me, Reverend. He isn't as strong as he seems. Tom's just a great big baby about stuff like this."

Ernest's shoulders shook. When he finally looked at me, rivers of tears ran down his face.

"Tom is resilient. He was a boxer, right? You don't need to worry about him. Let's look after you first, okay?"

I took his hands in mine.

"How long have you known?"

"Only a couple of weeks. I thought it was indigestion. Tom's cooking can be a little rough on my bowels sometimes." He winced.

I stroked his arm. "Does it hurt much?"

He shook his head. "It's not too bad."

Examining the lines on his face, I didn't believe him.

"Ernest, shall we pray?"

*****

I officiated the harvest service in slow motion. Every word waited longer on my lips. Every note of every hymn hung in the air, unable to escape St. Bridget's stone walls. I drifted through the coffee morning in the hall, shaking hands and making the right noises. Phil and Barbara packed up the offerings on the altar into boxes for distribution. I forced myself to laugh at their jokes. Life must go on.

I checked the pews for stray hymn books and locked the doors. Lawrence had joined Phil and Barbara at the front of the church. I wanted to run into his arms, but I struggled to put one foot in front of the other.

Soon they too would know about Ernest and feel the same aching foreboding that was crippling my heart. But for now, I had sworn not to tell anyone. To respect his wishes was the least I could do.

Barbara pushed Lawrence forward. He reached for my hand.

Don't propose now. Not here. Not today...

"Jess," he began.

Barbara tittered behind him. "Go on, she won't bite."

Lawrence scowled. "I'm trying! Jess—"

"He's bought you a weekend trip to Paris. Over Halloween. I've made sure your diary is clear. Oh, it's so romantic!"

What's Next for Reverend Jess?

SACRED SLAYING

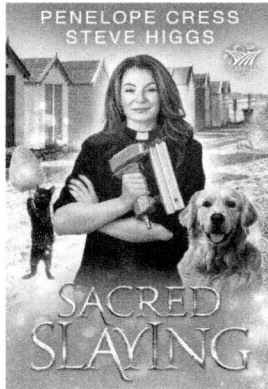

It's been nine months since Rev Jess Ward returned to the island of her birth. Nine crazy months of uncovering her family's pagan history, her own psychic gifts, and a veritable cornucopia of secrets and lies.

Is it too much to hope that her first Halloween on Wesberrey will pass without incident?

Of course it is.

When tragedy strikes the island's close-knit community on the night when the veil between heaven and earth is at its thinnest, Jess needs her family more than ever. But although she is surrounded by those who love her, Jess has never felt so alone.

Join Rev Jess Ward as she discovers her true identity and learns how to harness her new knowledge to root out those with murderous intent.

About the Author

P enelope lives on an island off the coast of Kent, England, with her four children and an elderly Jack Russell Terrier. A lover of murder mystery and cups of tea (served with a stack of digestive biscuits), she writes quaint cosy mysteries and other feel-good stories from a corner table in the vintage tea shop on the high street. Penelope loves nostalgia and all things retro. Her taste in music is also very last century.

Find out more about Penelope at www.penelopecress.com.

Want to know more?

G reenfield Press is the brainchild of bestselling author Steve Higgs. He specializes in writing fast paced adventurous mystery and urban fantasy with a humorous lilt. Having made his money publishing his own work, Steve went looking for a few 'special' authors whose work he believed in.

Georgia Wagner was the first of those, but to find out more and to be the first to hear about new releases and what is coming next, you can join the Facebook group by copying the following link into your browser www.facebook.com/GreenfieldPress.

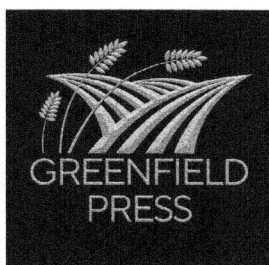

More Books By Steve Higgs

Blue Moon Investigations
Paranormal Nonsense
The Phantom of Barker Mill
Amanda Harper Paranormal Detective
The Klowns of Kent
Dead Pirates of Cawsand
In the Doodoo With Voodoo
The Witches of East Malling
Crop Circles, Cows and Crazy Aliens
Whispers in the Rigging
Bloodlust Blonde – a short story
Paws of the Yeti
Under a Blue Moon – A Paranormal
Detective Origin Story
Night Work
Lord Hale's Monster
The Herne Bay Howlers
Undead Incorporated
The Ghoul of Christmas Past
The Sandman
Jailhouse Golem
Shadow in the Mine
Ghost Writer

Felicity Philips Investigates
To Love and to Perish
Tying the Noose
Aisle Kill Him
A Dress to Die For
Wedding Ceremony Woes

Patricia Fisher Cruise Mysteries
The Missing Sapphire of Zangrabar
The Kidnapped Bride
The Director's Cut
The Couple in Cabin 2124
Doctor Death
Murder on the Dancefloor
Mission for the Maharaja
A Sleuth and her Dachshund in Athens
The Maltese Parrot
No Place Like Home

Patricia Fisher Mystery Adventures
What Sam Knew
Solstice Goat
Recipe for Murder
A Banshee and a Bookshop
Diamonds, Dinner Jackets, and Death
Frozen Vengeance
Mug Shot
The Godmother
Murder is an Artform
Wonderful Weddings and Deadly
Divorces
Dangerous Creatures

Patricia Fisher: Ship's Detective Series
The Ship's Detective
Fitness Can Kill
Death by Pirates
First Dig Two Graves

Albert Smith Culinary Capers
Pork Pie Pandemonium
Bakewell Tart Bludgeoning
Stilton Slaughter
Bedfordshire Clanger Calamity
Death of a Yorkshire Pudding
Cumberland Sausage Shocker
Arbroath Smokie Slaying
Dundee Cake Dispatch
Lancashire Hotpot Peril
Blackpool Rock Bloodshed
Kent Coast Oyster Obliteration
Eton Mess Massacre
Cornish Pasty Conspiracy

Realm of False Gods
Untethered magic
Unleashed Magic
Early Shift
Damaged but Powerful
Demon Bound
Familiar Territory
The Armour of God
Live and Die by Magic
Terrible Secrets

Printed in Great Britain
by Amazon